EXIT HER TRUE LOVE

Betty gained control of herself and began to explain. "You see," she said to Jane, "they were determined I should marry a man I can't *endure*, and when I wouldn't they tried to *trick* me into it anyway. I never suspected until I got into the church and looked around and couldn't see Bessemer anywhere; only the other one with his evil eyes gloating over me, and then I knew. They thought they would get me there before all that church full of people and I wouldn't dare do anything. But when I realized it, I just dropped right down in the aisle. I couldn't stand up, I was so frightened."

"But I don't understand," said Jane. "Were there *two* men?"

"Oh, yes," sighed Betty, "there were two."

"Well, where was the other one, the one you *wanted* to marry?"

"I-I don't know . . ."

Bantam Books by Grace Livingston Hill
Ask your bookseller for the books you have missed

Exit Betty

Grace Livingston Hill

BANTAM BOOKS
TORONTO · NEW YORK · LONDON · SYDNEY · AUCKLAND

*This low-priced Bantam Book
has been completely reset in a type face
designed for easy reading, and was printed
from new plates. It contains the complete
text of the original hard-cover edition.*
NOT ONE WORD HAS BEEN OMITTED.

EXIT BETTY

*A Bantam Book / published by arrangement with
Harper & Row, Publishers, Inc.*

PRINTING HISTORY
J. P. Lippincott edition published 1920.

Bantam edition / January 1986

ISBN 0-553-25459-6

Published simultaneously in the United States and Canada

---

*Bantam Books are published by Bantam Books, Inc. Its trade-
mark, consisting of the words "Bantam Books" and the por-
trayal of a rooster, is Registered in U.S. Patent and Trademark
Office and in other countries. Marca Registrada. Bantam
Books, Inc., 666 Fifth Avenue, New York, New York 10103.*

PRINTED IN THE UNITED STATES OF AMERICA

H   0 9 8 7 6 5 4 3 2 1

Exit Betty

Chapter 1

The crowd gave way and the car glided smoothly up to the curb at the canopied entrance to the church. The blackness of the wet November night was upon the street. It had rained at intervals all day.

The pavements shone wetly like new paint in the glimmer of the street lights, and rude shadows gloomed in every cranny of the great stone building.

Betty, alone in the midst of her bridal finery, shrank back from the gaze of the curious onlookers, seeming very small, like a thing of the air caught in a mesh of the earth.

She had longed all day for this brief respite from everyone, but it had passed before she could concentrate her thoughts. She started forward, a flame of rose for an instant in her white cheeks, but gone as quickly. Her eyes reminded one of the stars among the far-away clouds on a night of fitful storm, with only glimpses of their beauty in breaks of the overcast sky. Her small hands gripped one another excitedly, and the sweet lips were quivering.

A white-gloved hand reached out to open the car door, and other hands caught and cared for the billow of satin and costly lace with which she was surrounded, as if it, and not she, were the important one.

They led her up the curtained way, where envious eyes peeped through a furtive rip in the canvas, or craned around an opening to catch a better glimpse of her loveliness, one little dark-eyed foreigner even reached out a

1

grimy, wondering finger to the silver whiteness of her train; but she, all unknowing, trod the carpeted path as in a dream.

The wedding march was just beginning. She caught the distant notes, felt the hush as she approached the audience, and wondered why the ordeal seemed so much greater now that she had actually come to the moment. If she had known it would be like this—! Oh, why had she given in!

The guests had risen and were stretching their necks for the first vision of her. The chaplet of costly blossoms sat upon her brow and bound her wedding veil floating mistily behind, but the lovely head was bowed, not lifted proudly as a bride's should be, and the little white glove that rested on the arm of the large florid cousin trembled visibly. The cousin was almost unknown until a few hours before. His importance overpowered her. She drooped her eyes and tried not to wish for the quiet, gray-haired cousin of her own mother. It was so strange for him to have failed her at the last moment, when he had promised long ago to let nothing hinder him from giving her away if she should ever be married. His telegram, "Unavoidably detained," had been received but an hour before. He seemed the only one of her kind, and now she was all alone. All the rest were like enemies, although they professed deep concern for her welfare; for they were leagued together against all her dearest wishes, until she had grown weary in the combat.

She gave a frightened glance behind as if some intangible thing were following her. Was it a hounding dread that after all she would not be free after marriage?

With measured tread she passed the long white-ribboned way, under arches that she never noticed, through a sea of faces that she never saw, to the altar smothered in flowers and tropical ferns. It seemed interminable. Would it never end? They paused at last, and she lifted frightened eyes to the florid cousin, and then to the face of her bridegroom!

It was a breathless moment, and but for the deep tones of the organ now hushing for the ceremony, one of almost audible silence. No lovelier bride had trod those aisles in many a long year; so exquisite, so small, so young—and so exceeding rich! The guests were entranced, and every eye was greedily upon her as the white-robed minister advanced with his open book.

"Beloved, we are met together tonight to join this man—"

At that word they saw the bride suddenly, softly sink before them, a little white heap at the altar, with the white face turned upward, the white eyelids closed, the long dark lashes sweeping the pretty cheek, the wedding veil trailing mistily about her down the aisle, and her big bouquet of white roses and maidenhair ferns clasped listlessly in the white-gloved hand.

For a moment no one stirred, so sudden, so unexpected it was. It all seemed an astonishing part of the charming spectacle. The gaping throng with startled faces stood and stared. Above the huddled little bride stood the bridegroom, tall and dark and frowning, an angry red surging through his handsome face. The white-haired minister, with two red spots on his fine scholarly cheeks, stood grave with troubled dignity, as though somehow he meant to hold the little still bride responsible for this unseemly break in his beautiful service. The organ died away with a soft crash of the keys and pedals as if they too leaped up to see; the scent of the lilies swept sickeningly up in a great wave on the top of the silence.

In a moment all was confusion. The minister stooped, the best man sprang into the aisle and lifted the flowerlike head. Someone produced a fan, and one of the ushers hurried for a glass of water. A physician struggled from his pew across the laps of three stout dowagers, and knelt, with practiced finger on the little fluttering pulse. The bride's stepmother roused to solicitous and anxious attention. The organ came smartly up again in a hopeless tangle of chords and modulations. People climbed upon their seats to see, or crowded out in the aisle curiously and unwisely kind, and in the way. Then the minister asked the congregation to be seated; and amid the rustle of wedding finery into seats suddenly grown too narrow and too low, the ushers gathered up the little inert bride and carried her behind the palms across a hall and into the vestry room. The stepmother and a group of friends hurried after, and the minister requested the people to remain quietly seated for a few minutes. The organist by this time had recovered his poise and was playing soft tender melodies, but the excited audience was not listening.

"I thought she looked ghastly when she came in," declared the mother of three frowsy daughters. "It's strange she didn't put on some rouge."

"Um-mm! What a pity! I suppose she isn't strong! What did her own mother die of?" murmured another speculatively, preparing to put forth a theory before anyone else got ahead of her.

"Oh! The poor child!" sympathized a romantic friend. "They've been letting her do too much! Didn't they make a handsome couple? I'm crazy to see them come marching down the aisle. They surely wouldn't put off the wedding just for a faint, would they?"

And all over the church some woman began to tell how her sister's child, or her brother's niece, or her nephew's aunt had fainted just before her wedding or during it, till it began to seem quite a common performance, and one furnishing a unique and interesting part of the program for a wedding ceremony.

Meanwhile on a couch in the big gloomy vestry room lay Betty with a group of attendants about her. Her eyes were closed, and she made no move. She swallowed the aromatic ammonia that someone produced, and she drew her breath a little less feebly, but she did not open her eyes, nor respond when they spoke to her.

Her stepmother stooped over finally and spoke in her ear:

"Elizabeth Stanhope! Sit up and control yourself!" she said sharply in a low tone. "You are making a spectacle of yourself that you can never get over. Your father would be ashamed of you if he were here!"

It was the one argument that had been held a successful lash over her poor little quivering heart for the last five years, and Betty flashed open her sorrowful eyes and looked around on them with a troubled concentration as if she were just taking in what had happened.

"I'm so tired!" she said in a little weary voice. "Won't you just let me get my breath a minute?"

The physician nodded emphatically toward the door and motioned them out:

"She'll be all right in just a minute. Step outside and give her a chance to get calm. She's only worn out with excitement."

She opened her eyes and looked furtively about the room. There was no one there, and the door was closed. She could hear them murmuring in low tones just beyond it. She looked wildly about her with a frantic thought of escape. The two windows were deeply curtained, giving a narrow glimpse of blank wall. She sprang softly to her feet and looked out. There was a stone pavement far below. She turned silently and tried a door. It opened into a closet overflowing with musty hymn books. She closed it quickly and slipped back to her couch just in time as the door opened and the doctor came back. She could catch a glimpse of the others through the hall open door, anxiously peering in. She gathered all her self-control and spoke:

"I'm all right now, Doctor," she said quite calmly. "Would you just ask them to send Bessemer here a minute?"

"Certainly." The doctor turned courteously and went back the door, half closing it and making her request in a low tone. Then her stepmother's excited sibilant whisper:

"Bessemer! Why, he isn't here! He went down to the shore last night."

"Sh-h-h!" came another voice, and the door was shut smartly.

Betty's eyes grew wide with horror as she lay staring at the closed door, and a cold numbness seemed to envelop her, clutching at her throat, her heart, and threatening to overwhelm her.

Bessemer not here! What could it mean? Her mind seemed unable to grasp and analyze the nameless fear that awaited her outside that door. In a moment more they would all swarm in and surround her, and begin to clamor

for her to go back into that awful church—and *she could
not!*—EVER! She would far rather die!

She sprang to her feet again and glided noiselessly to the
only remaining uninvestigated door in the room. If this was
another closet she would shut herself inside and stay till she
died. She had read tales of people dying in a small space
from lack of air. At least, if she did not die she could stay
here till she had time to think. There was a key in the lock.
Her fingers closed around it and drew it stealthily from the
keyhole, as she slid through the door, drawing her rich satin
gown ruthlessly after. Her fingers were trembling so that
she scarcely could fit the key in the lock again and turn it,
and every click of the metal, every creak of the door,
sounded like a gong in her ears. Her heart was fluttering
wildly and the blood seemed to be pouring in torrents behind her eardrums. She could not be sure whether there
were noises in the room she had just left or not. She put her
hand over her heart, turned with a sickening dread to look
about her prison, and behold, it was not a closet at all, but a
dark landing to a narrow flight of stone steps that wound
down out of sight into the shadows. With a shudder she
gathered her white gown about her and crept down the
murky way, frightened, yet glad to creep within the friendly
darkness.

There were unmistakable sounds of footsteps overhead
now, and sharp exclamations. A hand tried the door above
and rattled it violently. For an instant her heart beat frightfully in her throat at the thought that perhaps after all she
had not succeeded in quite locking it, but the door held,
and she flew on blindly down the stairs, caring little where
they led only so that she might hide quickly before they
found the janitor and pried that door open.

The stairs ended in a little hall and a glass door. She
fumbled wildly with the knob. It was locked, but there was
a key! It was a large one and stuck, and gave a great deal of
trouble in turning. Her fingers seemed so weak!

Above the noises grew louder. She fancied the door was
open and the whole churchful of people were after her. She
threw her full weight with fear in the balance, and the key

turned. She wrenched it out of the rusty keyhole, slid out shutting the door after her, and stooping, fitted in the key again. With one more Herculean effort she locked it and stood up, trembling so that she could scarcely keep her balance. At least she was safe for a moment and could get her breath. But where could she go? She looked about her. High walls arose on either hand, with a murky sky above. A stone walk filled the space between and ran down the length of the church to a big iron gate. The lights of the street glistened fitfully on the puddles of wet in the depressions of the paving stones. The street looked quiet, and only one or two people were passing. Was that gate locked also, and if so could she ever climb it, or break through? Somehow she must! She shuddered at the thought of what would happen if she did not get away at once. She strained at the buttons on her soft white gloves and pulled the fingers off, slipping her hands out and letting the glove hands hang limp at her wrists. Then with a quick glance backward at a flicker of light that appeared wavering beyond the glass door, she gathered her skirts again and fled down the long stone walk. Silently, lightly as a ghost she passed, and crouched at the gate as she heard footsteps, her heart beating so loudly it seemed like a bell calling attention to her. An old man was shuffling past, and she shrank against the wall, yet mindful of the awful glass door back at the end of the narrow passage. If they should come now she could not hope to elude them!

She stooped and studied the gate latch. Yes, it was a spring lock, and had no key in it. Stealthily she tried it and found to her relief that it swung open. She stepped around it and peered out. The gateway was not more than a hundred feet from the brightly lighted corner of the main avenue where rows of automobiles were lined up waiting for the wedding ceremony to be over. She could see the chauffeurs walking back and forth and chatting together. She could hear the desultory wandering of the organ, too, from the partly open window near by. A faint sickening waft of lily sweetness swept out, mingled with a dash of drops from the maple tree on the sidewalk. In a panic she stepped forth and drew back again, suddenly realizing for the first time what it would be to go forth into the streets clad in her wedding garments. How could she do it and get away? It could not be done!

Down the street, with a backward, wistful glance at the church, hurried a large woman with a market basket. Her curious eyes shone in the evening light and darkness of the street. There was something about her face that made Betty know instantly that this woman would love to tell how she had seen her, would gather a crowd in no time and pursue her. She shrank farther back, and then waited in awful fear and tried to listen again. Was that a rattling at the glass door? She must get away no matter what happened! Where? Was there an alleyway or anything across the block? Could she hope to cross the street between the shadows unnoticed?

She looked out fearfully once more. A girl of her own age was approaching around the corner, paddling along in rubbers, and a long coat. She was chewing gum. Betty could see the outline of a strong good-natured jaw working contentedly as she was silhouetted against the light. She had her hands in her pockets, and a little dark hat worn boyishly on the back of her head, and she was humming a popular song. Betty had slipped behind the half open gate again and was watching her approach, her desperation driving her to thoughts that never would have entered her mind at another time. Suddenly, as the girl passed directly in front of the gate, Betty leaned forward and plucked at her sleeve:

"Wait!" she said sharply; and then, with a pitiful pleading in her voice, "Won't you help me just a minute, please?"

Chapter 2

The girl came to a standstill abruptly and faced about, drawing away just a hairbreath from the detaining hand, and surveying her steadily, the boyish expression in her eyes changing to an amused calculation such as one would fancy a cowboy held up on his native plains by a stray lamb might have worn.

"What's the little old idea!" asked the girl coldly, her eyes narrowing as she studied the other girl in detail and attempted to classify her into the known and unknown quantities of her world. Her face was absolutely expressionless as far as any sign of interest or sympathy was concerned. It was like a house with the door still closed and a well-trained butler in attendance.

"I've got to get away from here at once before anybody sees me," whispered Betty excitedly, with a fearful glance behind her.

"Do you want me to call a cab for you?" sneered the girl on the sidewalk, with an envious glance at the white satin slippers.

"Oh, no! Never!" cried Betty, wringing her hands in desperation. "I want you to show me somewhere to go out of sight, and if you will I'd like you to walk a block or so with me so I won't be so—so conspicuous! I'm so frightened I don't know which way to go."

"What do you want to go at all for?" asked the girl bluntly, with the look of an inquisitor, and the intolerance of the young for its contemporary of another social class.

9

"Because I *must!*" said Betty with terror in her voice. "They're coming! Listen! Oh, help me quick! I can't wait to explain!"

Betty dashed out of the gate and would have started up the street but that a strong young arm came out like a flash and a firm young fist gripped her arm like a vise. The girl's keen ears had caught a sound of turning key and excited voices, and her quick eyes pierced the darkness of the narrow court and measured the distance back.

"Here! You can't go togged out like that!" she ordered in quite a different tone. She flung off her own long coat and threw it around the shrinking little white figure, then knelt and deftly turned up the long satin draperies out of sight and fixed them firmly with a pin extracted from somewhere about her person. Quickly she stood up and pulled off her rubbers, her eye on the long dark passageway whence came now the decided sound of a forcibly opened door and footsteps.

"Put these on, quick!" she whispered, lifting first one slippered foot and then the other and supporting the trembling Betty in her strong young arms, while she snapped on the rubbers.

Lastly, she jerked the rakish hat from her own head, crammed it down hard over the orange-wreathed brow and gave her strange protégée a hasty shove.

"Now beat it around that corner and wait till I come!" she whispered, and turning planted herself in an idle attitude just under the church window, craning her neck and apparently listening to the music. A second later an excited usher, preceded by the janitor, came clattering down the passageway.

"Have you seen anyone go out of this gate recently?" asked the usher.

The girl, hatless and coatless in the chill November night, turned nonchalantly at the question, surveyed the usher coolly from the point of his patent leather shoes to the white gardenia in his buttonhole, gave his features a cursory glance, and then shook her head.

"There might have been an old woman come out a while back. Dressed in black, was she? I wasn't paying much attention. I think she went down the avenue," she said, and stretched her neck again, standing on her tiptoes to view the wedding guests. Her interest suddenly became real, for she spied a young man standing in the church, in full view of the window, back against the wall with his arms folded, a fine handsome young man with pleasant eyes and a head like that of a young nobleman, and she wanted to make sure of his identity. He looked very much like the young lawyer whose office boy was her "gentleman friend." Just to make sure she gave a little spring from the sidewalk that brought her eyes almost on a level with the window and gave her a brief glimpse, enough to see his face quite clearly; then she turned with satisfaction to see that the janitor and the usher had gone back up the passageway, having slammed the gate shut. Without more ado the girl wheeled and hurried down the street toward the corner where Betty crouched behind a tree trunk, watching fearfully for her coming.

"Aw! You don't need to be that scared!" said the girl, coming up. "They've gone back. I threw 'em off the scent. Come on! We'll go to my room and see what to do. Don't talk! Somebody might recognize your voice. Here, we'll cut through this alley and get to the next block. It's further away and not so many folks passing."

Silently they hurried through the dark alley and down the next street, Betty holding the long cloak close that no gleam of her white satin might shine out and give away her secret, her heart beating like a trip-hammer in her breast, her eyes filled with unshed tears, the last words of her stepmother ringing in her ears. Was she making her father ashamed? Her dear dead father! Was she doing the wrong thing? So long that thought had held her! But she could not go back now. She had taken an irrevocable step.

Her guide turned another corner abruptly and led her up some stone steps to the door of a tall, dingy brick house, to which she applied a latchkey.

The air of the gloomy hall was not pleasant. The red wallpaper was soiled and torn, and weird shadows flickered from the small gas taper that blinked from the ceiling. There were suggestions of old dinners, stale fried potatoes, and pork in all the corners, and one movement toward the stairs seemed to stir them up and set them going again like old memories.

The stairs were bare and worn by many feet, and not particularly clean. Betty paused in dismay, then hurried on after her hostess, who was mounting up, one, two, three flights, to a tiny hall bedroom at the back. A fleeting fear that perhaps the place was not respectable shot through her heart, but her other troubles were so great that it found no lodgment. Panting and trembling she arrived at the top and stood looking about her in the dark, while the other girl found a match and lighted another wicked little flickering gas burner.

Then her hostess drew her into the room and closed and locked the door. As a further precaution she climbed upon a chair and pushed the transom shut.

"Now," she said with a sigh of evident relief, "we're safe! No one can hear you here, and you can say what you please. But first we'll get this coat and hat off and see what's the damage."

As gently as if she were undressing a baby the girl removed the hat and coat from her guest, and shook out the wonderful shining folds of satin. It would have been a study for an artist to have watched her face as she worked, smoothing out wrinkles, shaking the lace down and uncrushing it, straightening a bruised orange blossom, and putting everything in place. It was as if she herself were an artist restoring a great masterpiece, so silently and absorbedly she worked, her eyes full of a glad wonder that it had come to her once to be near and handle anything so rare and costly. The very touch of the lace and satin evidently thrilled her; the breath of the exotic blossoms was nectar as she drew it in.

Betty was still panting from her climb, still trembling from her flight, and she stood obedient and meek while the other girl pulled and shook and brushed and patted her into shape again. When all was orderly and adjusted about the crumpled bride, the girl stood back as far as the limits of the tiny room allowed and surveyed the finished picture.

"There now! You certainly do look great! That there band of flowers round your forehead makes you look like some queen. 'Coronet'—ain't that what they call it? I read that once in a story at the Public Library. Say! Just to think I should pick that up in the street! Good night! I'm glad I came along just then instead o' somebody else! This certainly is some picnic! Well, now, give us your dope. It must've been pretty stiff to make you cut and run from a show like the one they got up for you! Come, tune up and let's hear the tale. I rather guess I'm entitled to know before the curtain goes up again on this little old stage!"

The two tears that had been struggling with Betty for a long time suddenly appeared in her eyes and drowned them out, and in dismay she brought out a faint little sorry giggle of apology and amusement and dropped on the tiny bed, which filled up a good two-thirds of the room.

"Good night!" exclaimed the hostess in alarm, springing to catch her. "Don't drop down that way in those glad rags! You'll finish 'em! Come, stand up and we'll get 'em off. You look all in. I'd oughta known you would be!" She lifted Betty tenderly and began to remove her veil and unfasten the wonderful gown. It seemed to her much like helping an angel remove her wings for a nap. Her eyes shone with genuine pleasure as she handled the hooks deftly.

"But I've nothing else to put on!" gurgled Betty helplessly.

"I have!" said the other girl.

"Oh!" said Betty with a sudden thought. "I wonder! Would you be willing to exchange clothes? Have you perhaps got some things you don't need that I could have, and I'll give you mine for them? I don't suppose perhaps a wedding dress would be very useful unless you're thinking of getting married soon, but you could make it over and use it for the foundation of an evening dress—"

The other girl was carefully folding the white satin skirt at the moment, but she stopped with it in her arms and sat down weakly on the foot of the bed with it all spread out in her lap and looked at her guest in wonder.

"You don't mean you *wantta give it up!*" she said in an awed tone. "You don't mean you would be willing to take some of my old togs for it?"

"I certainly would!" cried Betty eagerly. "I never want to see these things again! *I hate* them! And besides, I want to get away somewhere. I can't go in white satin! You know that! But I don't like to take anything of yours that you might need. Do you think these things would be worth anything to you? You weren't thinking of getting married yourself sometime soon, were you?"

"Well, I might," said the other girl, looking self-conscious. "I got a gentleman friend. But I wasn't expectin' to get in on any trooso like this!" She let her finger move softly over the satin hem as if she had been offered a plume of the angel's wing. "Sure, I'll take it off you if I've got anything you're satisfied to have in exchange. I wouldn't mind havin' it to keep jest to look at now and then and know it's mine. It'd be somethin' to live for, jest to know you had that dress in the house!"

Suddenly Betty, without any warning even to herself, dropped upon her knees beside the diminutive bed and began to weep. It seemed somehow so touching that a thing like a mere dress could make a girl glad like that. All the troubles of the days that were past went over her in a great wave of agony, and overwhelmed her soul. In soft silk and lace petticoat and camisole with her pretty white arms and shoulders shaking with great sobs she buried her face in the old patchwork quilt that her hostess had brought from her village home, and gave way to a grief that had been long in growing. The other girl now thoroughly alarmed, laid the satin on a chair and went over to the little stranger, gathering her up in a strong embrace, and gradually lifting her to the bed.

"You poor little kid, you! I oughtta known better! You're just all in! You ben gettin' ready to be married, and something big's been troubling you, and I bet they never gave you any lunch—er else you wouldn't eat it—and you're just natcheraly all in. Now you lie right here an' I'll make you some supper. My name's Jane Carson, and I've got a good mother out to Ohio, and a nice home if I'd had sense enough to stay in it; only I got a chanct to make big money in a fact'ry. But I know what 'tis to be lonesome, an' I ain't hardhearted, if I do know how to take care of misself. There! There!"

She smoothed back the lovely hair that curled in golden tendrils where the tears had wet it.

"Say, now, you needn't be afraid! Nobody'll getcha here! I know how to bluff 'em. Even if a policeman should come after yeh, I'd get around him somehow, and I don't care what you've done or ain't done, I'll stand by yeh. I'm not one to turn against anybody in distress. My mother always taught me that. After you've et a bite and had a cup of my nice tea with cream and sugar in it you'll feel better, and we'll have a real gabfest and hear all about it. Now, you just shut your eyes and wait till I make that tea."

Jane Carson thumped up the pillow scientifically to make as many of the feathers as possible and shifted the little flower head upon it. Then she hurried to her small washstand and took a little iron contrivance from the drawer, fastening it on the sickly gas jet. She filled a tiny kettle with water from a faucet in the hall and set it to boil. From behind a curtain in a little box nailed to the wall she drew a loaf of bread, a paper of tea and a sugar bowl. A cup and saucer and other dishes appeared from a pasteboard box under the washstand. A small shelf outside the tiny window yielded a plate of butter, a pint bottle of milk, and two eggs. She drew a chair up to the bed, put a clean handkerchief on it, and spread forth her table. In a few minutes the fragrance of tea and toast pervaded the room, and water was bubbling happily for the eggs. As easily as if she had a chum to dine with her she sat down on the edge of the bed and invited her guest to supper. As she poured the tea she wondered what her colaborers at the factory would think if they knew she had a real society lady visiting her. It wasn't every working girl that had a white satin bride thrust upon her suddenly this way. It was like a fairy story, having a strange bride lying on her bed, and everything a perfect mystery about her. She eyed the white silk ankles and dainty slippers with satisfaction. Think of wearing underclothes made of silk and real lace!

It seemed to Betty as if never before in all her life had she tasted anything so delicious as that tea and toast and softboiled egg cooked by this wonderful girl on a gaslight and served on a chair. She wanted to cry again over her gladness at being here. It didn't seem real after all the trouble she had been through. It couldn't last! Oh, of course it couldn't last!

This thought came as she swallowed the last bite of toast, and she sat up suddenly!

"I ought to be doing something quick!" she said in sudden panic. "It is getting late and I must get away. They'll be watching the trains, perhaps. I ought to have gone at once. But I don't know where I can go. Give me some old things, please. I must get dressed at once."

"Lie down first and tell me who you are and what it's all about. I can't do a thing for you till I know. I've got to go into this with my eyes open or I won't stir one step," she declared stubbornly.

Betty looked at her with wide eyes of trouble and doubt. Then the doubt suddenly cleared away, and trust broke through.

"I can trust you, I'm sure! You've been so good to me! But it seems dreadful to tell things about my family, even to one who has been so kind. My father would be so hurt—"

"Your father? Where is your father? Why didn't he take care of you and keep you from getting into such big trouble, I'd like to know?"

The blue eyes clouded with tears again.

"My father died five years ago," she said, "but I've always tried to do as he would want to have me do. Only—this—I *couldn't.*"

"H'm!" said Jane Carson. "Then he prob'ly wouldn't of wanted you to. Suppose you take the rest of those togs off. I'll find you a warm nightgown and we'll get to bed. It's turning cold here. They take the heat off somewhere about

six o'clock in the evening, and it gets like ice up here sometimes."

Jane shivered and went to her small trunk, from which
she produced a coarse but clean flannelette nightgown, and
Betty, who had never worn anything but a dainty lingerie
one before in all her life, crept into it thankfully and cuddled down with a warm feeling that she had found a real
friend. It was curious why she did not shrink from this poor
girl, but she did not, and everything looked clean and nice.
Besides, this was a wonderful haven of refuge in her dire
necessity.

Chapter 3

Meanwhile, in the stately mansion that Betty had called home, a small regiment of servants hastened with the last tasks in preparation for the guests that were soon expected to arrive. The great rooms had become a dream of paradise, with silver rain and white lilies in a mist of soft green depending from the high ceilings. In the midst of all, a fairy bower of roses and tropical ferns created a nook of retirement where everyone might catch a glimpse of the bride and groom from any angle in any room. The spacious vistas stretched away from an equally spacious hallway, where a wide and graceful staircase curved up to a low gallery, smothered in flowers and palms and vines; and even so early the musicians were taking their places and tuning their instruments. On the floor above, where room after room shone in beauty, with costly furnishings, and perfect harmonies, white-capped maids flitted about, putting last touches to dressing tables and pausing to gossip as they passed one another:

"Well, 'twill all be over soon," sighed one, a wan-faced girl with discontented eyes. "Ain't it kind of a pity, all this fuss just for a few minutes?"

"Yes, an' glad I'll be!" declared another, a fresh young Irish girl with a faint, pretty brogue. "I don't like the look of my Lady Betty. A pretty fuss Candace her old nurse would be makin' if she was here the night! I guess the madam knew what she was about when she give her her walkin' ticket! Candace never could bear them two boys, and *him* was the worse of the two, she always said."

"Well, a sight of good it would do for old Candace to make a fuss!" said the discontented one. "And anyhow, he's as handsome as the devil, and she's got money enough, so she oughtn't complain."

"Money ain't everything!" sniffed Aileen. "I wouldn't marry a king if I wasn't crazy about him!"

"Oh, you're young!" sneered Marie with disdain. "Wait till your looks go! You don't know what you'd take up with!"

"Well I'd never take up with the likes of *him*!" returned the Irish girl grandly, "and what's more he knows it!" She tossed her head meaningfully and was about to sail away on her own business when a stir below stairs attracted their attention. A stout, elderly woman, dressed in a stiff new black silk and an outrageous hat, came panting up the stairs looking furtively from side to side, as if she wished to escape before anyone recognized her.

"It's Candace!" exclaimed Aileen. "As I live! Now what d'ye wantta know about that! Poor soul! Poor soul! Candy! Oh!—Candy! What iver brought ye here the night? This is no place for the loikes of you. You better beat it while the beatin' is good if ye know which side yer bread's buttered!"

But the old nurse came puffing on, her face red and excited:

"Is she here? Has she come yet, my poor wee Betty?" she besought them eagerly.

"Miss Betty's at the church now gettin' married!" announced Marie uppishly, "and you'd best be gettin' out of here right away, for the wedding party's due to arrive any minute now and madam'll be very angry to have a servant as doesn't belong snoopin' round at such a time!"

"Be still, Marie! For shame!" cried Aileen. "You've no need to talk like that to a self-respectin' woman as has been in this house more years than you have been weeks! Come along, Candace, and I'll slip you in my room and tell you all about it when I can get away long enough. You see, Miss Betty's being married——"

"But she's *not*!" cried Candace wildly. "I was at the church myself. Miss Betty sent me the card to be sure and come, and where to sit and all, so she'd see me; and I went, and she come up the aisle as white as a lily and dropped right there before the poolpit, just like a little white lamb that couldn't move another step, all of a heap in her pretty things! And they stopped the ceremony and everybody got up, and they took her away, and we waited till pretty soon the minister said the bride wasn't well enough to proceed with the ceremony and would they all go home, and I just slipped out before the folks got their wraps on and took a side street with wings to my feet and got up here! Haven't they brought her home yet, the poor wee thing? I been thinkin' they might need me yet, for many's the time I've brought her round by my nursin'."

The two maids looked wildly at one another, their glances growing into incredulity, the eyebrows of Marie moving toward her well-dressed hair with a lofty disapproval.

"Well, you'd better come with me, Candy," said Aileen drawing the excited old servant along the hall to the back corridor gently. "I guess there's some mistake somewheres; anyway, you better stay in my room till you see what happens. We haven't heard anything yet, and they'd likely send word pretty soon if there's to be a change in the program. You say she fell——?"

But just then sounds of excitement came distantly up to them and Aileen hastened back to the gallery to listen. It was the voice of Madam Stanhope angrily speaking to her youngest son.

"You must get Bessemer on the phone at once and order him home! I told you it was a great mistake sending him away. If he had been standing there, where she could see him, everything would have gone through just as we planned it——"

"Aw! Rot! Mother. Can't you shut up? I know what I'm about and I'm going to call up another detective. Bessemer may go to the devil for all I care! How do you know but he has, and taken her with him? The first thing to do is to get that girl back! You ought to have had more sense than to show your whole hand to my brother. You might have known he'd take advantage——"

Herbert Hutton slammed into the telephone booth under the stairs and Madam Stanhope was almost immediately aware of the staring servants who were trying not to seem to have listened.

Mrs. Stanhope stood in the midst of the beautiful empty rooms and suddenly realized her position. Her face froze into the haughty lines with which her menage was familiar, and she was as coldly beautiful in her exquisite heliotrope gown of brocaded velvet and chiffon with the glitter of jewels about her smooth plump neck, and in her carefully waved black hair as if she were quietly awaiting the bridal party instead of facing defeat and mortification.

"Aileen, you may get Miss Betty's room ready to receive her. She has been taken ill and will be brought home as soon as she is able to be moved," she announced, without turning an eyelash. "Put away her things, and get the bed ready!" One could see that she was thinking rapidly. She was a woman who had all her life been equal to an emergency, but never had quite such a tragic emergency been thrust upon her to camouflage before.

"James!" catching the eye of the butler, "there will be no reception tonight, of course, and you will see that the hired people take their things away as soon as possible, and say that I will agree to whatever arrangements they see fit to make, within reason, of course. Just use your judgment, James, and by the way, there will be telephone calls, of course, from our friends. Say that Miss Betty is somewhat better, and the doctor hopes to avert a serious nervous breakdown, but that she needs entire rest and absolute quiet for a few days. Say that and nothing more, do you understand, James?"

The butler bowed his thorough understanding and Madam Stanhope sailed nobly up the flower-garlanded staircase, past the huddled musicians, to her own apartment. Aileen, with a frightened glance, scuttled past the door as she was closing it.

"Aileen, ask Mr. Herbert to come to my room at once when he has finished telephoning, and when Mr. Bessemer arrives send him to me at once!" Then the door closed and the woman was alone with her defeat, and the placid enameled features melted into an angry snarl like an animal at bay. In a moment more Herbert stormed in.

"It's all your fault, Mother!" he began, with an oath. "If you hadn't dragged Bessemer into this thing I'd have had her fixed. I had her just about where I wanted her, and another day would have broken her in. She's scared to death of mental hospitals, and I told her long ago that it would be dead easy to put a woman in one for life. If I had just hinted at such a thing she'd have married me as meek as a lamb!"

"Now look here, Bertie," flared his mother excitedly, "you've got to stop blaming me! Haven't I given in to you all your life, and now you say it's all my fault the least little thing that happens! It was for your sake that I stopped you; you know it was. You couldn't carry out any such crazy scheme. Betty's almost of age, and if those trustees should find out what you had threatened, you would be in jail for life, and goodness knows what would become of me."

"Trustees! How would the trustees find it out?"

"Betty might tell them."

"Betty might *not* tell them, not if she was *my wife*!" He bawled out the words in a way that revealed no blissful future to the one who should have the misfortune to become his wife. "I think I'd have her better trained than that. As for you, Mother, you're all off, as usual! What do you think could possibly happen to *you*? You're always saying you do everything for me, but when it comes right down to brass tacks I notice you're pretty much of a selfish coward on your own account."

For a moment the baffled woman faced her angry uncontrolled son in speechless rage, then gathered command of the situation once more, an inscrutable expression on her hard-lined face. Her voice took on an almost pitiful reproach as she spoke in a low, even tone that could hardly fail to bring the instant attention of her spoiled son.

"Bertie, you don't know what you're talking about!" she said, and there was a strained white look of fear about her mouth and eyes as she spoke. "I'm going to tell you, in this great crisis, what I did for you, what I risked that you might enjoy the luxury which you have had for the last five years. Listen! The day before Mr. Stanhope died he wrote a letter to the trustees of Betty's fortune giving very explicit directions about her money and her guardianship, tying things up so that not one cent belonging to her should pass through my hands, which would have left us with just my income as the will provided, and would have meant comparative poverty for us all except as Betty chose to be benevolent. I kept a strict watch on all his movements those last few days, of course, and when I found he had given Candace a letter to mail, I told her I would look after it, and I brought it up to my room and read it, for I suspected just some such thing as he had done. He was very fussy about Betty and her rights, you remember, and he had always insisted that this was Betty's house, her mother's wedding present from the grandfather, and therefore not ours at all, except through Betty's bounty. I was determined that we should not be turned out of here, and that you should not have to go without the things you wanted while that child had everything and far more than she needed. So I burned the letter! Now, do you see what the mother you have been blaming has done for you?"

But the son looked back with hard glittering eyes and a sneer on his handsome lustful lips:

"I guess you did it about as much for your own sake as mine, didn't you?" he snarled. "And I don't see what that's got to do with it, anyway. Those trustees don't know what they missed if they never got the letter, and you've always kept in with them, you say, and made them think you were crazy about the girl. They pay you Betty's allowance till she's of age, don't they? They can't lay a finger on you. You're a fool to waste my time talking about a little thing like that when we ought to be planning a way to get hold of that girl before the trustees find out about it. If we don't get her fixed before she's of age we shall be in the soup as far as the property is concerned. Isn't that so? Well, then, we've got to get her good and married——"

"If you only had let her marry Bessemer quietly," whimpered his mother, "and not have brought in all this deception. It will look so terrible if it ever comes out. I shall never be able to hold up my head in society again——!"

"There you are again! Thinking of yourself——!" sneered the dutiful son, getting up and stamping about her room like a wild man. "I tell you, Mother, that girl is *mine*, and I won't have Bessemer or anybody else interfering. *She's mine!* I told her so a long time ago, and she knows it! She can't get away from me, and it's going to go the harder with her because she's tried. I'm never going to forgive her making a fool out of me before all those people! I'll get her yet! Little fool!"

Herbert was well on his way into one of those fits of uncontrollable fury that had always held his mother in obedience to his slightest whim since the days when he used to lie on the floor and scream himself black in the face and hold his breath till she gave in; and the poor woman, wrought to the highest pitch of excitement already by the tragic events of the evening, which were only the climax of long weeks of agitation, anxiety, and plotting, dropped suddenly into her boudoir chair and began to weep.

But this new manifestation on the part of his usually pliable mother only seemed to infuriate the young man. He walked up to her, and seizing her by the shoulder, shook her roughly.

"Cut that out!" he said hoarsely. "This is no time to cry. We've got to make some kind of a plan. Don't you see we'll have the hounds of the press at our heels in a few hours? Don't you see we've got to make a plan and stick to it?"

His mother looked up, regardless for once of the devastation those few tears had made of her carefully groomed face, a new terror growing in her eyes.

"I've told James to answer all telephone calls and say that Betty is doing as well as could be expected, but that the doctor says she must have perfect quiet to save her from a nervous breakdown——" she answered him coldly. "I'm not quite a fool if you do think so——"

"Well, that's all right for tonight, but what'll we say tomorrow if we don't find her——"

"Oh! She'll come back," said the stepmother confidently. "She can't help it. Why, where would she go? She hasn't a place on earth since she's lost confidence in that cousin of her mother's because he didn't come to her wedding. She hasn't an idea that he never got her note asking him to give her away. Thank heaven I got hold of that before it reached the postman! If that old fussbudget had been here we should have had trouble indeed. I had an experience with him once just before I married Betty's father, and I never want to repeat it. But we must look out what gets in the papers!"

"It's rather late for that, I suspect. The bloodhounds 'll be around before many minutes and you better think up what you want said. But I'm not so sure she wouldn't go there, and we better tell the detectives that. What's the old guy's address. I'll call him up long-distance and say she was on a motoring trip and intended to stop there if she had time. I'll ask if she's reached there yet."

"That's a good idea, although I'm sure she was too hurt about it to go to him. She cried all the afternoon. It's a wonder she didn't look frightful! But that's Betty! Cry all day and come out looking like a star without any paint either. It's a pity somebody that would have appreciated it couldn't have had her complexion."

"That's you all over, Mother, talking about frivolous things when everything's happening at once. You're the limit! I say, you'd better be getting down to business! I've thought of another thing. How about that old nurse, Candace? Betty used to be crazy about her. What became of her?"

Mrs. Stanhope's face hardened, and anxiety grew in her eyes.

"She might have gone to her, although I don't believe she knows where she is. I'm sure I don't. I sent her away just before we began to get ready for the wedding. I didn't dare have her here. She knows too much and takes too much upon herself. I wouldn't have kept her so long, only she knew I took the trustee's letter, and she was very imprudent about it once or twice, so that I didn't really dare to let her go until just a few days ago. I thought things would all be over here before she could do any harm and Betty would be of age and have her money in her own right, and being your wife, of course there wouldn't be any more trouble about it."

"Well, you better find out what's become of her!" said the young man with darkening face. "*She* ought to be locked up somewhere! She's liable to make no end of trouble! You can't tell what she's stirred up already! Ring for a servant and find out if they know where she is. Ten to one that's where Betty is."

Mrs. Stanhope, with startled face, stepped to the hall and summoned Aileen:

"Aileen, have you any idea where we could find Miss Betty's old nurse, Candace?" she asked in a scathing tone, studying the maid's countenance. "I think it might be well to send for her in case Miss Betty needs her. She was so much attached to her!"

Aileen lifted startled eyes to her mistress' face. There was reserve and suspicion in her glance.

"Why, she was here a few minutes ago," she said guardedly. "It seems Miss Betty sent her an invitation, and when Miss Betty took sick she was that scared she ran out of the church and come here to find out how she was. She might not have gone yet. I could go see."

"Here! Was she here?" Mrs. Stanhope turned her head to her son and her eyes said: "That's strange!" but she kept her face well under control.

"Yes, you might go and see if you can find her, Aileen, and if you do, tell her I would like to see her a moment."

Aileen went away on her errand and Mrs. Stanhope turned to her son.

"Betty can't have gone to her unless there was some collusion. But in any case I think we had better keep her here until we know something."

Quick trotting steps were heard hurrying along the hall and a little jerky knock announced unmistakably the presence of Candace.

Mrs. Stanhope surveyed the little red-faced creature coolly and sharply:

"Candace, you have broken one of my express commands in returning here without permission from me, but seeing it was done in kindness I will overlook it this time and let you stay. You may be useful if they bring my daughter home tonight and I presume she will be very glad to see you. Just now she is—umm——" she glanced furtively at her son, and lifting her voice a trifle, as if to make her statement more emphatic—"she is at a private hospital near the church where they took her till she should be able to come home. It will depend on her condition whether they bring her tonight or tomorrow or in a few days. Meantime, if you like you may go up to your old room and wait until I send for you. I shall have news soon and will let you know. Don't go down to the servants' quarters, I wish to have you where I can call you at a moment's notice."

Candace gave her ex-mistress a long, keen suspicious stare, pinned her with a glance as steely as her own for an instant, in search of a possible ulterior motive, and then turning on her little fat heel, vanished like a small fast racer in the direction of her old room.

"Now," said Mrs. Stanhope, turning with a sigh of relief, "she's safe! I'll set Marie to watch her and if there's anything going on between those two Marie will find out."

But Herbert Hutton was already sitting at his mother's desk with the telephone book and calling up long distance.

All the long hours when he had expected to have been standing under the rose bower downstairs in triumph with his bride, Herbert Hutton sat at that telephone in his mother's boudoir alternately raging at his mother and shouting futile messages over the phone. The ancient cousin of Betty's mother was discovered to be seriously ill in a hospital and unable to converse even through the medium of his nurse, so there was nothing to be gained there. Messages to the public functionaries in his town developed no news. Late into the night, or rather far toward the morning, Bessemer was discovered at a cabaret where his persistent mother and brother had traced him, too much befuddled with his evening's carouse to talk connectedly. He declared Betty was a good old girl, but she might go to thunder for all he cared; he knew a girl "worth twice of her."

His mother turned with disgust from his babbling voice, convinced that he knew nothing of Betty's whereabouts. Nevertheless, by means of a financial system of threats and rewards which she had used on him successfully for a number of years, she succeeded in impressing upon him the necessity of coming home at once, and just as the pink was beginning to dawn in the gray of the morning, Bessemer drove up in a hired car, and stumbled noisily into the house, demanding to know where the wedding was. He wanted to kiss the bride.

Candace, still in her stiff black silk, stood in the shadowy hall, as near as she dared venture, and listened, with her head thoughtfully on one side. Betty in her note about the wedding had said she was going to be married to Bessemer. But Bessemer didn't sound like a bridegroom. Had Bessemer run away then, or what? But some things looked strange. She remembered that Aileen had spoken as if Hebert was the bridegroom, but she had taken it for a rare slip of the tongue and thought nothing of it. When Aileen next came that way, she asked her if she happened to have got hold of one of the invitations, and Aileen, with her finger on her lips, nodded, and presently returned with something under her apron:

"I slipped it from the wastebasket," she said, "and Miss Betty got a holt of it, and there was a tremenjus fuss about something, I couldn't make out what; but I heard the missus say it was all a mistake as she gave the order over the phone, and she must have misspoke herself, but anyhow she thought she'd destroyed them all and given a rush order and they would be all right and sent out in plenty of time. So she sticks this back in the wastebasket and orders me to take the basket down and burn it, but I keeps this out and hides it well. I couldn't see nothin' the matter with it, can you?"

"There's *all* the matter with it!" declared the angry nurse as she glared at the name of Herbert Hutton thoughtfully, and read between the lines more than she cared to tell.

Chapter 4

Not two miles away, Betty lay safe and warm in the flannelette nightgown, and watched Jane Carson turn out the light and open the window. A light leaped up from the street and made a friendly spot of brightness on the opposite wall, and Betty had a sense of coziness that she had not felt since she was in boarding school with a roommate.

"Now," said Jane, climbing into bed and pulling up the covers carefully lest she should let the cold in on her guest, "let's hear!—You warm enough?"

There was a curious tenderness in her voice as if she had brought home a young princess and must guard her carefully.

"Oh, perfectly!" said Betty, giving a little nervous shiver. "And I'm so glad to be here safe away from them all! Oh, I've needed someone to advise me so much! I haven't had a soul since they sent my old nurse away because she dared to take my part sometimes."

Suddenly Betty buried her face in the pillow and began to sob and Jane reached out quick gentle arms and gathered her in a close comforting embrace. In a moment more Betty had gained control of herself and began to explain:

"You see," she said, catching her breath bravely, "they were determined I should marry a man I can't *endure*, and when I wouldn't they tried to *trick* me into it anyway. I never suspected until I got into the church and looked around and couldn't see Bessemer anywhere; only the other one with his evil eyes gloating over me, and then I knew! They thought they would get me there before all that church full of people and I wouldn't dare do anything. But when I realized it, I just dropped right down in the aisle. I couldn't stand up, I was so frightened."

"But I don't understand," said Jane. "Were there *two* men?"

"Oh, yes," sighed Betty, "there were two."

"Well, where was the other one, the one you *wanted* to marry?"

"I don't know——" said Betty with a half sob in her voice. "That's just what frightened me. You see they were my stepmother's two sons, and it was my father's dying wish that I should marry one of them. I didn't really *want* to marry Bessemer, but I simply *loathed* Herbert, the younger one, who was so determined to marry me. I was terribly afraid of him. He had been frightfully cruel to me when I was a child and when we grew up he was always tormenting me; and then when he tried to make love to me he was so repulsive that I couldn't bear to look at him. It really made me sick to think of ever marrying him. Oh—I wouldn't—no matter who asked me. So Bessemer and I decided to get married to stop the trouble. They were always nagging him, too, and I was kind of sorry for him."

"But why should you marry anybody you didn't want to, I'd like to know!" exclaimed Jane in horror. "This is a free country and nobody ever makes people marry anybody they don't like anymore. Why didn't you just beat it?"

"I thought about that a good many times," said Betty, pressing her tired eyes with her cold little fingers, "but I couldn't bring myself to do it. In the first place, I didn't know where to go, nor what to do. They never would let me learn to do anything useful, so I couldn't have got any work; and anyhow I had a feeling that it wouldn't be possible to get away where Herbert couldn't find me if he wanted to. He's that way. He always gets what he wants, no matter whom it hurts. He's *awful*—Jane—really!"

There was a pitiful note in her voice that appealed to the mother in Jane, and she stooped over her guest and patted her comfortingly on the shoulder:

"You poor little kid," she said tenderly, "you must have been worried something awful, but still I don't get you; what was the idea in sticking around and thinking you *had* to marry somebody you didn't like? You coulda gone to someone and claimed pertection. You could uv appealed to the p'lice if worst came to worse——!"

"Oh! But Jane I couldn't! That would have brought our family into disgrace, and Father would have felt so *dreadfully* about it if he had been alive! I couldn't quite bring myself, either, to go against his dying request. We had always been so much to each other, Daddy and I. Besides, I didn't mind *Bessemer so much*—he was always kind—though we never had much to do with each other——"

"Well, I don't think I'd have stopped around long to please a father that didn't care anymore for me than to want me to marry somebody I felt that way about!" said Jane, indignantly. "I haven't much use for a father like that!"

"Oh, but he wasn't like that!" said Betty, rising up in her eagerness and looking at Jane through her shining curls that were falling all about her eager, troubled young face, "and he did love me, Jane, he loved me better than anything else in the whole world! That was why I was willing to sacrifice almost anything to please him."

"Well, I'll be darned!" said Jane Carson, sitting up squarely in bed and staring at the spot of light on the wall. "That gets my goat! How could a man love you and yet want to torment you?"

"Well, you see, Jane, he hadn't been very fond of them when they were boys"—she spoke it with dignity and a little gasp as if she were committing a breach of loyalty to explain, but realized that it was necessary—"and he felt when he was dying that he wanted to make reparation, so he thought if I should marry one of them it would show them that he had forgiven them——"

"It—may—be—so," drawled Jane slowly, nodding her head deliberately with each word, "but—I don't see it that *way*! What kind of a man was this father of yours, anyway?"

"Oh, a wonderful man, Jane!" Betty eagerly hastened to explain. "He was all the world to me, and he used to come

up to school weekends and take me on beautiful trips and
we had the best times together, and he would tell me about
my own dear mother——"

Betty's hand grasped Jane's convulsively and her voice
died out, in a sudden sob. Jane's hand went quickly to the
bright head on the pillow:

"There! there!" she whispered tenderly, "don't take on so,
I didn't mean anything, I was just trying to dope it out; get
it through my bean what in thunder——! Say! Did *he* TELL
you he wanted you to marry those guys?"

"Oh, no, he left word—it was his dying request."

"Who'd he request it to?"

"My stepmother."

"H'm! I thought so! How'd you know he did? How'd you
know but she was lyin'?"

"No," said Betty sorrowfully, "she wasn't lying, she
showed me the paper it was written on. There couldn't be
any mistake. And his name was signed to it, his dear handwriting, just as he always wrote it with the little quirl to the
S that wasn't like anybody else. It went through me just like
a knife when I saw it, that my dear father should have asked
me to do what was so very very hard for me to think of. It
was so much harder to have it come that way. If he had only
asked me himself and we could have talked it over, perhaps
he would have helped me to be strong enough to do it, but
to have *her* have to *tell me*! She felt that herself. She tried to
be kind, I think. She said she wanted to have him wake me
up and tell me himself, but she saw his strength was going
and he was so anxious to have her write it down quick and
let him sign it that she did as he asked——"

"Well, you may depend on it he never wrote it at all—or
anyhow, never knew what he was signing. Like as not she
dragged it out of him some way while he was out of his mind
or so near dying he didn't know what he was about. Besides, they mightta some of 'em forged his name. It's easy to
copy signatures. Lotsa people do it real good. If I was you I
wouldn't think another mite about it. If he was a man like
you say he is, he couldn'ta done a thing like that to his own
little girl, not on his life! It ain't like real fathers and moth-

ers to. I know, fer I've got a mother that's a peach and no mistake! No, you may depend on it, he never knew a thing about that, and marrying a guy like that is the last thing on earth he'd want you to do."

"Oh, do you really think so? Oh, are you *sure*?" cried Betty, clinging to Jane eagerly, the tears raining down her white cheeks. "I've thought so a thousand times, but I didn't dare trust myself to decide."

"Yes, I'm sure!" said Jane, gathering her in her arms and hugging her tight, just as she would have done with a little sister who had waked up in the night with a bad dream. "Now, look here, you stop crying and don't you worry another bit. Just tell me the rest if there's any rest, so I'll know what to bank on. Who is the other guy, the one you didn't mind marryin'? What became of him?"

"Why, that's the queer part," said Betty, troubled again. "He didn't seem to be anywhere, and when they carried me into the room back of the church and fanned me and got water to bathe my face, a doctor came and gave me some medicine and sent them all out, and I asked him to send Bessemer to me. I wanted to find out why he hadn't been standing up there by the minister the way I expected. I heard the doctor go out and ask for Bessemer and I heard my stepmother's voice say, 'Why Bessemer isn't here! He's gone down to the shore!' and then somebody said, 'Hush,' and they shut the door, and I was so frightened that I got up and tried all the doors till I found one that led down some stairs, and I locked it behind me and ran and found you!"

"You poor little kid!" cried Jane, cuddling her again. "I sure am glad I was on the job! But now, tell me, what's your idea? Will they make a big noise and come huntin' you?"

"Oh, yes!" said Betty wearily. "I suppose they will. I *know* they will in fact. Herbert won't be balked in anything he wants——Bessemer won't count. He never counts. I'm sort of sorry for him, though I don't like him much. You see they had been making an awful fuss with him, too, about some actress down at the shore that he was sending flowers to, and I knew he didn't have a very easy time. So when he came in one day and asked me why I didn't marry *him* and settle the whole thing that way, I was horrified at first, but I finally thought perhaps that would be the best thing to do. He said he wouldn't bother me any, if I wouldn't bother him; and we thought perhaps the others would let us alone then. But I might have known Herbert wouldn't give in! Bessemer is easily led—Herbert could have hired him to go away tonight—or they may have *made* him ask me to marry him. He's like that," she said sadly. "You can't depend on him. I don't know. You see, it was kind of queer about the invitations. They came with Herbert's name in them first, and my stepmother tried to keep me from seeing them. She said they were late and she had them all sent off; but I found one, and when I went to my stepmother with it she said it was a mistake. She hadn't meant me to be annoyed by seeing it; and she didn't know how it happened; she must have misspoken herself—but it had been corrected and they would rush it through and send them right from the store this time so there wouldn't be any delay. I tried to think it was all right, but it troubled me, for I saw that Herbert hadn't given up at all—though he pretended to go away, and I hoped I wouldn't have any more trouble—but I might have known! Herbert never gave up anything in his life, not Even when Father was living. He always managed to get his way, somehow——"

"Did he love you so much?" Jane asked awesomely.

Betty shuddered.

"Oh, I don't know whether it was love or hate! It was all the same. I hate to think about him—he is—*unbearable*, Jane! Why, Jane, once he told me if he ever got me in his power he'd break my will or kill me in the attempt!"

"Well, now, there, kid! Don't you think another bit about him, the old brute! You just lie down and sleep as easy as if you was miles away. They won't any of 'em ever find you here with me, and I've pulled the washstand in front of the door, so you needn't be dreaming of anybody coming in and finding you. Now go to sleep, and tomorrow I'll sneak you away to a place where they can't ever find you. Good night, kid!" and Jane leaned down and kissed the soft hair on the pillow beside her. Betty flung her arms about her newfound friend and kissed her tenderly:

"Oh, you've been so good to me! What should I ever have done if I hadn't found you. You were like an angel. I think surely God must have sent you to help me."

"I shouldn't wonder if He did!" said Jane thoughtfully. "An angel in a mackintosh! Some angel!"

Jane Carson with her eyes wide open lay staring into the darkness and thinking it all over. She did not waste much time marveling over the wonder that it had all happened to her. That would do for afterward when there was nothing else to be done about it. Now there must be some plans made and she was the one to make them. It was quite plain that the wonderful and beautiful Elizabeth Stanhope, the plans for whose wedding had been blazoned in the papers for days beforehand, was not at present capable of making or carrying out anything effective. Jane was. She knew it. She was a born leader and promoter. She liked nothing better than to work out a difficult situation. But this was the most difficult proposition that she had ever come up against. When her father died and her mother was left with the little house and the three younger children to support in a small country village, and only plain sewing and now and then a boarder to eke out a living for them all, she had sought and found, through a summer visitor who had taught her Sunday school class for a few weeks, a good position in this big eastern city. She had made good and been promoted until her wages not only kept herself with strict economy, but justified her in looking forward to the time when she might send for her next younger sister. Her deft fingers kept her meager wardrobe in neatness—and a tolerable deference to fashion, so that she had been able to annex the "gentleman friend" and take a little outing with him now and then at a moving picture theater or a Sunday evening service. She had met and vanquished the devil on more than one battlefield in the course of her experience with different department heads; and she was wise beyond her years in the ways of the world. But this situation was different. Here was a girl who had been brought up "by hand," as she would have said with a sneer a few hours before, and she would have despised her for it. She raised up on one elbow and leaned over once more to watch the delicate profile of this gentle maiden, in the dim fitful light of the city night that came through the one little window. There had been something appealing in the beauty and frankness of the girl-bride, something appalling in the situation she had found herself in. Jane Carson didn't know whether she was doing right or not to help this stray bride. It made her catch her breath to think how she might be bringing all the power of the law and of money upon her reckless young head, but she meant to do it, just the same.

Elizabeth Stanhope! What a beautiful name! It fitted right in with all the romance Jane had ever dreamed. If she only could write scenarios, what a thriller this would make!

Then she lay down and fell to planning.

Chapter 5

The morning dawned, and still no word from the missing bride. But the brief guarded sentences which Herbert Hutton had telephoned to the newspapers had been somehow sidetracked, and in their place a ghastly story had leaked out which some poor, hard pressed reporter had gleaned from the gossip in the church and hurried off to put into type before there was time for it to be denied. Hotfoot the story had run, and great headlines proclaimed the escape of Betty even while the family was carefully paving the way for the report of a protracted illness and absence, if need be, till they could find trace of her. The sun rose brightly and made weird gleaming of the silver wire on which the dying roses hung. The air was heavy with their breath, and the rooms in the early garish light looked out of place as if some fairy wand had failed to break the incantation at the right hour and left a piece of magicland behind. The parlor maid went about uncertainly, scarcely knowing what to do and what to leave undone, and the milk cars, and newsboys, and early laborers began to make a clatter of every day on the streets. The morning paper, flung across the steps with Betty's picture, where Betty's reluctant feet had gone a few hours before, seemed to mock at life, and upstairs the man that Betty thought she went out to marry, lay in a heavy stupor of sleep. Happy Betty, to be resting beneath the coarse sheet of the kindly working girl, sleeping the sleep of

38

exhaustion and youth in safety, two miles from the rose-bowered rooms!

Long before day had really started in the great city Jane Carson was up and at work. She dressed swiftly and silently, then went to her little trunk, and from it selected a simple wardrobe of coarse clean garments. One needed mending and two buttons were off. She sat by the dingy window and strained her eyes in the dawn to make the necessary repairs. She hesitated long over the pasteboard suit box that she drew from under the bed. It contained a new dark blue serge dress for which she had saved a long time and in which she had intended to appear at church next Sabbath. She was divided between her desire to robe the exquisite little guest in its pristine folds and her longing to wear it herself. There was a sense of justice also which entered into the matter. If that elegant wedding dress was to be hers, and all those wonderful silk underclothes, which very likely she would never allow herself to wear, for they would be out of place on a poor working girl, it was not fair to repay their donor in old clothes. She decided to give the runaway bride her new blue serge. With just a regretful bit of a sigh she laid it out on the foot of the bed, and carefully spread out the tissue papers and folded the white satin garments away out of sight, finishing the bundle with a thick wrapping of old newspapers from a pile behind the door and tying it securely. She added a few pins to make the matter more sure, and got out a stub of a pencil and labeled it in large letters. "My summer dresses," then shoved it far back under the bed. If any seeking detective came he would not be likely to bother with that, and he might search her trunk in vain for white satin slippers and wedding veils.

Breakfast was next, and she put on her cloak and hurried out for supplies for the larder had been heavily depleted the night before to provide for her guest. With a tender glance toward the sleeper she slipped the key from the lock and placed it in the outside of the door, silently locking her guest within. Now there would be no danger of anyone spiriting her away while she was gone, and no danger that the girl might wake up and depart in her absence.

She stopped a newsboy on his way to the subway and bought a paper, thrilling at the thought that there might be something in it about the girl who lay asleep in her little hall bedroom.

While she waited for her bundles she stole a glance at her paper, and there on the front page in big letters ran the heading:

STANHOPE WEDDING HELD UP AT ALTAR BY UNCONSCIOUS BRIDE

Relatives Seek Runaway Girl Who Is Thought to Be Insane

She caught her breath and rolled the paper in a little wad, stuffing it carelessly into her pocket. She could not read anymore of that in public. She hastened back to her room.

Betty was still sleeping. Jane stood watching her for a full minute with awe in her face. She could not but recognize the difference between herself and this fine sweet product of civilization and wealth. With the gold curls tossed back like a ripple of sunshine, and a pathetic little droop at the corners of her sweet mouth, nothing lovelier could be. Jane hurried to the window and turned her back on the bed while she perused the paper, her rage rising at the theories put forth. It was even hinted that her mother had been insane. Jane turned again and looked hard at the young sleeper, and the idea crossed her mind that even she might be deceived. Still, she was willing to trust her judgment that this girl was entirely sane, and anyhow she meant to help her! She stuffed the paper down behind the trunk and began to get breakfast. When it was almost ready she gently awoke the sleeper.

Betty started at the light touch on her shoulder and looked wildly around at the strange room and stranger face of the other girl. In the dim light of the evening she had scarcely got to know Jane's face. But in a moment all the happenings of the day before came back, and she sat up excitedly.

"I ought to have got away before it was light," she said gripping her hands together. "I wonder where I could go, Jane?" It was pleasant to call this girl by her first name. Betty felt that she was a tower of strength, and so kind.

"I have this ring," she said, slipping off an exquisite diamond and holding it out. "Do you suppose there would be any way I could get money enough to travel somewhere with this? If I can't I'll have to walk, and I can't get far in a day that way."

Betty was almost lighthearted, and smiling. The night had passed and no one had come. Perhaps after all she was going to get away without being stopped.

Jane's face set grimly.

"I guess there won't be any walking for you. You'll have to travel regular. It wouldn't be safe. And you don't want no rich jewelry along either. Was that your wedding ring?"

"Oh, no; Father gave it to me. It was Mother's, but I guess they'd want me to use it now. I haven't anything else."

"Of course," said Jane shortly to hide the emotion in her voice. "Now eat this while I talk," thrusting a plate of buttered toast and a glass of orange marmalade at her, and hastening to pour an inviting cup of coffee.

"Now, I been thinking," she said sitting down on the edge of the bed and eating bits of the piece of toast she had burned—Betty's was toasted beautifully—"I got a plan. I think you better go to Ma. She's got room enough for you for awhile, and I want my sister to come over and take a place I can get fer her. If you was there she could leave. Mebbe you could help Ma with the kids. Of course we're poor and you ain't used to common things like we have them, but I guess you ain't got much choice in your fix. I got a paper this morning. They're huntin' fer you hotfoot. They say you was temperary insane, an' 'f I was you I'd keep out o' their way awhile. You lay low an' I'll keep my eye out and let you know. I've got a little money under the mattress I can let you have till that ring gets sold. You can leave it with me an' I'll do the best I can if you think you can trust me. Of course I'm a stranger, but then, land! So are you! We just *gotta* trust each other. And I'm sending you to my mother if you'll go!"

"Oh!" said Betty, springing up and hugging her impulsively, "you're so good! To think I should find somebody just like that right in the street when I needed you so. I almost think God did it!"

"Well, mebbe!" said Jane, in her embarrassment turning to hang up a skirt that had fallen from its hook. "That's what they say sometimes in Chrishun Deavor meetin'. Ever go to Chrishun Deavor? Better go when you get out home. They have awful good socials an' ice cream, and you'll meet some real nice folks. We've got a peach of a minister, and his wife is perfec'ly dandy. I tell you I missed 'em when I came to the city! They was always doing something nice fer the young folks."

"How interesting!" said Betty, wondering if she might really be going to live like other girls. Then the shadow of her danger fell over her once more, and her cheek paled. "If I can only get there safely." She shuddered. "Oh, Jane! You can't understand what it would be to have to go back!"

"Well, you're not going back. You're going to Tinsdale, and nobody's going to find you ever, unless you want 'em to! See? Now, listen! We haven't any time to waste. You oughtta get off on the ten o'clock train. I put out some clothes there for yeh. They ain't like yours, but it won't do fer you to go dressed like a millionairess. Folks out to Tinsdale would suspect yeh right off the bat. You gotta go plain like me, and it's this way: You're a friend I picked up in the city whose mother is dead and you need country air awhile, see? So I sent you home to stay with Ma till you got strong again. I'm wirin' Ma. She'll understand. She always does. I kinda run Ma anyhow. She thinks the sun rises an' sets in me, so she'll do just what I say."

"I'm afraid I oughtn't to intrude," said Betty soberly, taking up the coarse, elaborately trimmed lingerie with a curious look, and trying not to seem to notice that it was different from any she had ever worn before.

"Say! Looka here!" said Jane Carson facing round from her coffee cup on the washstand. "I'm sorry to criticize, but if you could just talk a little slang or something. Folks'll never think you belong to me. '*Intrude!*' Now, that sounds stuck up! You oughtta say 'be in the way,' or something natural like that. See?"

"I'm afraid I don't," said Betty dubiously, "but I'll try."

"You're all right, kid," said Jane with compunction in her voice. "Just let yourself down a little like I do, and remember you don't wear silk onderclothes now. I'm afraid those stockings won't feel very good after yours, but you gotta be careful. An' 'f I was you I'd cut my hair off, I really would. It's an awful pity, it's so pretty, but it'll grow again. How old are you?"

"Almost twenty-one," said Betty thoughtfully. "Just three months more and I'll be twenty-one."

"H'm! Of age!" said Jane with a sharp significant look at her, as if a new thought had occurred. "Well, you don't look it! You could pass for fifteen, especially if you had your hair bobbed. I can do it for you if you say so."

"All right," said Betty promptly without a qualm. "I always wanted it short. It's an awful nuisance to comb."

"That's the talk!" said Jane. "Say 'awful' a lot, and you'll kinda get into the hang of it. It sounds more—well, *natural*, you know; not like society talk. Here, sit down and I'll do it quick before you get cold feet. I sure do hate to drop them curls, but I guess it's best."

The scissors snipped, snipped, and the lovely strands of bright hair fell on the paper Jane had spread for them. Betty sat cropped like a sweet young boy. Jane stood back and surveyed the effect through her lashes approvingly. She knew the exact angle at which the hair should splash out on the cheek to be stylish. She had often contemplated cutting her own, only that her mother had begged her not to, and she realized that her hair was straight as a die and would never submit to being tortured into that alluring wave over the ear and out toward the cheekbone. But this sweet young thing was a darling! She felt that the daring deed had been a success.

"I got a bottle of stuff to make your hair dark," she remarked. "I guess we better put it on. That hair of yours is

kinda conspicuous, you know, even when it's cut off. It won't
do you any harm. It washes off soon." And she dashed
something on the yellow hair. Betty sat with closed eyes and
submitted. Then her mentor burnt a cork and put a touch to
the eyebrows that made a different Betty out of her. A soft
smudge of dark under her eyes and a touch of talcum
powder gave her a sickly complexion and when Betty stood
up and looked in the glass she did not know herself. Jane
finished the toilet by a smart though somewhat shabby
black hat pulled well down over Betty's eyes, and a pair of
gray cotton gloves, somewhat worn at the fingers. The high-
laced boots she put upon the girl's feet were two sizes too
large, and wobbled frightfully, but they did well enough,
and there seemed nothing more to be desired.

"Now," said Jane as she pinned on her own hat, "you've
gotta have a name to go by. I guess you better be Lizzie
Hope. It kinda belongs to yeh, and yet nobody'd recognize
it. You don't need to tell Ma anything you don't want to,
and you can tell her I'll write a letter tonight all about it.
Now come on! We gotta go on the trolley a piece. I don't see
havin' you leave from the general station. We'll go up to the
junction and get the train there."

With an odd feeling that she was bidding good-by to herself forever and was about to become somebody else, Betty
gave one more glance at the slim boylike creature in the
little mirror over the washstand and followed Jane out of the
room, shuffling along in the big high-heeled boots, quite
unlike the Betty that she was.

Chapter 6

Warren Reyburn laid down his pen and shoved back his office chair impatiently, stretching out his long muscular limbs nervously and rubbing his hands over his eyes as if to clear them from annoying visions.

James Ryan, his office boy and stenographer, watched him furtively from one corner of his eye, while his fingers whirled the typewriter on through the letter he was typing. James wanted to take his girl to the movies that evening and he hadn't had a chance to see her the day before. He was wondering if Mr. Reyburn would go out in time for him to call her up at her noon hour. He was a very temperamental stenographer and understood the moods and tenses of his most temperamental employer fully. It was all in knowing how to manage him. James was most deferential, and knew when to keep still and not ask questions. This was one of the mornings when he went to the dictionary himself when he wasn't sure of a word rather than break the ominous silence. Not that Mr. Reyburn was a hard master, quite the contrary, but this was James' first place straight from his brief course at business school, and he was making a big bluff of being an old experienced hand.

There was not much business to be done. This was Warren Reyburn's "first place" also in the world of business since finishing his law course, and he was making a big bluff at being very busy, to cover up a sore heart and an anxious mind. It was being borne in upon him gradually that he was not a shouting success in business so far. The rosy dreams that had floated near all through his days of hard study had one by one left him, until his path was now leading through a murky gray way with little hope ahead. Nothing but sheer grit kept him at it, and he began to wonder how long he could stick it out if nothing turned up.

True, he might have accepted an offer that even now lay open on his desk; a tempting offer, too, from a big corporation who recognized the influence of his old family upon their particular line of business; but it was a line that his father and his grandfather had scorned to touch, and he had grown up with an honest contempt for it. He just could not bring himself to wrest the living from the poor and needy, and plunder the unsuspecting, and he knew that was what it would be if he closed with this offer. Not yet had he been reduced to such depths, he told himself shutting his fine lips in a firm curve. No, not if he starved!

That was the legitimate worry that ruffled his handsome brow as he sat before his desk frowning at that letter. He meant to begin dictation on its answer in another five minutes or so, but meantime he was forcing himself to go over every point and make it strong and clear to himself, so that he should say, "No!" strongly and clearly to the corporation! It might do harm to make his reason for declining so plain, but he owed it to his self-respect to give it nevertheless, and he meant to do so. After all, he had no business so far to harm, so what did it matter? If nothing turned up pretty soon to give him a start he would have to change his whole plan of life and take up something else where one did not have to wait for a reputation before he could have a chance to show what was in him.

But underneath the legitimate reason for his annoyance this morning there ran a most foolish little fretting, a haunting discomfort.

He had taken his cousin to a wedding the night before because her husband had been called away on business, and she had no one to escort her. They had been late and the church was crowded. He had had to stand, and as he idly looked over the audience he suddenly looked full into the great sad eyes of the sweetest little bride he had ever seen. He had not been a young man to spend his time over pretty faces, although there were one or two nice girls in whom he was mildly interested. He had even gone so far as to wonder now and then which of them he would be willing to see sitting at his table day after day the rest of his life, and he had not yet come to a satisfactory conclusion. His cousin often rallied him about getting married, but he always told her it would be time enough to think about that when he had an income to offer her.

But when he saw that flower-face, his attention was held at once. Somehow he felt as if he had not known there was a face like that in all the world, so like a child's, with a frank yet modest droop to the head, and the simplicity of an angel, yet the sadness of a sacrificial offering. Unbidden, a great desire sprang up to lift for her whatever burden she was bearing, and bring light into those sad eyes. Of course it was a passing sensation, but his eyes had traveled involuntarily to the front of the church to inspect the handsome forbidding face of the bridegroom, and with instant dissatisfaction he looked back to the girl once more and watched her come up to the altar, speculating as those who love to study humanity are wont to do when they find an interesting subject. How had those two types ever happened to come together? The man's part in it was plain. He was the kind who go about seeking whom they may devour, thought Warren Reyburn. But the woman! How could a wise-eyed child like that have been deceived by a handsome face? Well, it was all speculation of course, and he had nothing to do with any of them. They were strangers to him and probably always would be. But he had no conception at that time what a small world he lived in, nor how near the big experiences of life lie all about us.

He watched the lovely bride as all the audience watched her until he saw her fall, and then he started forward without in the least realizing what he was doing. He found himself half way up the side aisle to the altar before he came to himself and forced his feet back to where his cousin was sitting. Of course he had no right up there, and what could he do when there were so many of her friends and relatives about her?

His position near the side door through which they carried her made it quite possible for him to look down into her still face as they took her to the vestry room, and he found a great satisfaction in seeing that she was even more beautiful at close hand than at a distance. He wondered afterward why his mind had laid so much stress upon the fact that her skin was lovely like a baby's without any sign of cosmetics. He told himself that it was merely his delight to learn that there was such a type, and that it ran true.

He was therefore not a little disappointed that the minister, after the congregation had waited an unconscionable time for the return of the bride, came out and announced that owing to her continued collapse the ceremony would have to be postponed. The clatter of polite wonder and gossip annoyed him beyond measure, and he was actually cross with his cousin on the way home when she ranted on about the way girls nowadays were brought up, coddled, so that a breath would blow them away. Somehow she had not looked like that kind of a girl.

But when the morning papers came out with sensational headlines proclaiming that the bride had run away, and suggesting all sorts of unpleasant things about her, he felt a secret exultation that she had been brave enough to do so. It was as if he had found that her spirit was as wise and beautiful as her face had been. His interest in the matter exceeded all common sense and he was annoyed and impatient with himself more than he cared to own. Never before had a face lured his thoughts like this one. He told himself that his business was getting on his nerves, and that as soon as he could be sure about one or two little matters that he hoped would fall into his hands to transact, he would take a few days off and run down to the shore.

Again and again the little white bride came across his vision and thoughts, and hindered the courteous but stinging phrases with which he had intended to illumine his letter. At last he gave it up and taking his hat went out in the keen November air for a walk to clear his brain.

This was James Ryan's opportunity. It was almost twelve o'clock and no harm in calling the "forelady" in the cotton blouse department of the big factory. He swung to the telephone with alacrity.

"I want to speak with Miss Carson, please. Yes, Miss J. Carson. Is that Miss Carson? Oh, hello, Jane, is that you?"

"Yes, it is *Mister* Ryan," answered Jane sweetly.

"Jane!"

"Well, didn't you 'Miss Carson' me?"

"Give it up, Jane. You win. Say, Jane!"

"Well, Jimmie?"

"That's my girl, say how about that wedding veil? Been thinking any more about it?"

There was silence for a moment, then a conscious giggle, the full significance of which James Ryan was not in a position to figure out.

"Say, Jimmie, quit your kiddin'! You mustn't say things like that over the phone."

"Why not?"

"'Cause. Folks might listen."

"I should worry! Well, since you say so. How about seein' a show together tonight?"

"Fine an' dandy, Jimmie! I'll be ready at the usual time. I gotta go now, the boss is comin'. So long, Jimmie!"

"So long, darling!"

But the receiver at the other end hung up with a click, while Jane with a smile on her lips thought of the pasteboard box under her bed and wondered what Jimmie would say if he could know. For Jane had fully made up her mind that Jimmie was not to know. Not at present, anyhow. Sometime she might tell him if things turned out all right, but she knew just what lordly masculine advice and criticism would lie upon James Ryan's lips if she attempted to tell him about her strange and wonderful guest of the night before. Maybe she was a fool to have trusted a stranger that way. Maybe the girl would turn out to be insane or wrong somehow, and trouble come, but she didn't believe it; and anyhow, she was going to wait, until she saw what happened next before she got Jimmie mixed up in it. Besides, the secret wasn't hers to tell. She had promised Betty, and she always kept her promises. That was one reason why she was so slow in promising to think about a wedding veil in response to James Ryan's oft repeated question.

That evening on the way to the movies Jane instituted an investigation.

"Jimmie, what kind of a man is your boss?"

"White man!" said Jimmie promptly.

"Aw! Cut it out, James Ryan! I don't mean how'd 'e look, or what color is he; I mean what kind of a *man* is he?"

"Well, that's the answer. White man! What's the matter of that? I said it and I meant it. He's white if there ever was one!"

"Oh, that" said Miss Carson is scorn. "Of course I know he's a peach. If he wasn't you wouldn't be workin' for him. What I mean, is he a *snob*?"

"No chance!"

"Well, I saw him *with* 'em last night. I was passin' that big church up Spruce Street and I saw him standin' with his arms folded so——" she paused on the sidewalk and indicated his pose. "It was a swell weddin' and the place was full up. He had a big white front an' a clawhammer coat. I know it was him 'cause I took a good look at him that time you pointed him out at church that evenin'. I wondered was he *in with* them swells?"

Her tone expressed scorn and not a little anxiety, as if she had asked whether he frequented places of low reputation.

"Oh, if you mean, *could* he be, why that's a diffrunt thing!" said James the wise. "*Sure*, he could be if he wanted, I guess. He's got a good family. His uncle's some high muckymuck, and you often see his aunts' and cousins' names in the paper giving teas and receptions and going places. But he don't seem to go much. I often hear folks ask him why he wasn't some place last night, or phone to know if he won't come, and he always says he can't spare the time, or he can't affort it, or something like that."

"Ain't he rich, Jimmie?"

"Well, no, not exactly. He may have some money put away, or left him by someone. If he don't have I can't fer the life of me see how he lives. But he certainly don't get it in fees. I often wonder where my salary comes from, but it always does, regular as the clock."

"Jimmie, doesn't he have *any* business at all?"

"Oh, yes he has business, but it ain't the paying kind. Fer instance, there was a man in today trying to get his house back that another man took away from him, and my boss *took the case*! He took it *right off the bat* without waiting to see whether the man could pay him anything or not! He can't! He's only a poor laboring man, and a rich man stole his house. Just out an' out stole it, you know. It's how he got rich. Like as not we'll lose it, too, those rich men have so many ways of crawling out of a thing and making it look nice to the world. Oh, he'll get a fee, of course—twenty-five dollars, perhaps—but what's twenty-five dollars, and like as not never get even the whole of that, or have to wait for it? Why, it wouldn't keep *me* in his office long! Then there was a girl trying to get hold of the money her own father left her, and her uncle frittered away and pertends it cost him all that, and *he's* been supporting *her*! Well, we took that, too, and we won't get much out of that even if we do win. Then there come along one of these here rich guys with a pocket full of money and a nice slick tongue wanting to be protected from the law in some devilment, and *him* we *turned down flat*! That's how it goes in our office. I can't just figger out how it's coming out! But he's a good guy if there ever was one!"

"I should say!" responded Jane with shining eyes. "Say, Jimmie, what's the matter of us throwin' a little business in his way—real, payin' business, I mean?"

"Fat chance!" said Jimmie dryly.

"You never can tell!" answered Jane dreamily. "I'm goin' to think about it. Our fact'ry has lawyers sometimes. I might speak to the boss."

"Do!" said Jimmie sarcastically. "And have yer labor for yer pains! We'll prob'ly turn *them* down. Fact'ries are *always* doing things they hadn't ought to."

But Jane was silent and thoughtful, and they were presently lost in the charms of Mary Pickford.

The evening papers came out with pictures of Elizabeth Stanhope and her bridegroom that was to have been. Jane cut away the bridegroom and pasted the bride's picture in the flyleaf of her Bible, then hid it away in the bottom of her trunk.

Chapter 7

Whe n Betty found herself seated on the day coach of a way train, jogging along toward a town she had never seen and away from the scenes and people of her childhood, she found herself trembling violently. It was as if she had suddenly been placed in an airplane all by herself and started off to the moon without any knowledge of her motor power or destination. It both frightened and exhilarated her. She wanted to cry and she wanted to laugh, but she did neither. Instead she sat demurely for the first hour and a half looking out of a window like any traveler, scarcely turning her head nor looking at anything in the car. It seemed to her that there might be a detective in every seat just waiting for her to lift her eyes that he might recognize her. But gradually as the time dragged by and the landscape grew monotonous she began to feel a little more at her ease. Furtively she studied her neighbors. She had seldom traveled in a common car, and it was new to her to study all types as she could see them here. She smiled at a dirty baby and wished she had something to give it. She studied the careworn man and the woman in black who wept behind her veil and would not smile no matter how hard the man tried to make her. It was a revelation to her that any man would try as hard as that to make a woman smile. She watched the family with five children and nine bundles, and counted the colors on a smart young woman who got in at a way station. Every minute of the day was interesting. Every mile of dreary

November landscape that whirled by gave her more free-
dom.

She opened the little shabby handbag that Jane had given
her and got out the bit of mirror one inch by an inch and
half backed with pasteboard on which lingered particles of
the original green taffeta lining and studied her own strange
face, trying to get used to her new self and her new name.
Jane had written it, Lizzie Hope, on the back of the envelope containing the address of Mrs. Carson. It seemed
somehow an identification card. She studied it curiously
and wondered if Lizzie Hope was going to be any happier
than Betty Stanhope had been. And then she fell to thinking over the strange experiences of the last twenty-four
hours and wondering whether she had done right or not,
and whether her father would have been disappointed in
her, "ashamed of her," as her stepmother had said. Somehow Jane had made her feel that he would not, and she was
more lighthearted than she had been for many a day.

Late in the afternoon she began to wonder what Tinsdale would be like. In the shabby handbag was her ticket to
Tinsdale and eight dollars and a half in change. It made her
feel richer than she had ever felt in her life, although she
had never been stinted as to pocket money. But this was her
very own, for her needs, and nobody but herself to say how
she should spend either it or her time.

Little towns came in sight and passed, each one with one
or two churches, a schoolhouse, a lot of tiny houses. Would
Tinsdale look this way? How safe these places seemed, yet
lonely, too! Still, no one would ever think of looking for her
in a lonely little village.

They passed a big brick institution and she made out the
words, "State Hospital," and shuddered inwardly as she
thought of what Jane had told her about the morning paper.
Suppose they should hunt her up and *put her in a mental
hospital*, just to show the world that it had not been their
fault that she had run away from her wedding! The thought
was appalling. She dropped her head on her hand with her
face toward the window and tried to pretend she was asleep
and hide the tears that would come, but presently a boy

came in at the station with a big basket and she bought a ham sandwich and an apple. It tasted good. She had not expected that it would. She decided that she must have been pretty hungry and then fell to counting her money, aghast that the meager supper had made such a hole in her capital. She must be very careful. This might be all the money she would have for a very long time, and there was no telling what kind of an impossible place she was going to. She might have to get away as eagerly as she had come. Jane was all right, but that was not saying that her mother and sisters would be.

It was growing dark, and the lights were lit in the car. All the little babies had been given drinks of water, and strange things to eat, and tumbled to sleep across laps, on seats, anywhere they would stick. They looked so funny and dirty and pitiful with their faces all streaked with soot and molasses candy that somebody had given them. The mother looked tired and greasy and the father was fat and dark, with unpleasant black eyes that seemed to roll a great deal. Yet he was kind to the babies and his wife seemed to like him. She wondered what kind of a home they had, and what relation the young fellow with the shiny dark curls bore to them. He seemed to take as much care of the babies as did their father and mother.

The lights were flickering out in the villages now and gave a friendly inhabited look to the houses. Sometimes when the train paused at stations Betty could see people moving back and forth at what seemed to be kitchen tables and little children bringing dishes out, all working together. It looked pleasant and she wondered if it would be like that where she was going. A big lump of loneliness was growing in her throat. It was one thing to run away from something that you hated, but it was another to jump into a new life where one neither knew nor was known. Betty began to shrink inexpressibly from it all. Not that she wanted to go back! Oh, no; far from it! But once when they passed a little white cemetery with tall dark fir trees waving guardingly above the white stones she looked out almost wistfully. If she were lying in one of those beside her father and mother how safe and rested she would be. She wouldn't have to worry anymore. What was it like where Father and Mother had gone? Was it a real place? Or was that just the end when one died? Well, if she were sure it was all she would not care. She would be willing to just go out and not be. But somehow that didn't seem to be the commonly accepted belief. There was always a beyond in most people's minds, and a fear of just what Betty didn't know. She was a good deal of a heathen, though she did not know that either.

Then, just as she was floundering into a lot of theological mysteries of her own discovery the nasal voice of the conductor called out: "Tinsdale! Tinsdale!" and she hurried to her feet in something of a panic, conscious of her short hair and queer clothes.

Down on the platform she stood a minute trying to get used to her feet, they felt so numb and empty from long sitting. Her head swam just a little, too, and the lights on the station and in the houses near by seemed to dance around her weirdly. She had a feeling that she would rather wait until the train was gone before she began to search for her new home, and then when the wheels ground and began to turn and the conductor shouted "All aboard!" and swung himself up the step as she had seen him do a hundred times that afternoon, a queer sinking feeling of loneliness possessed her, and she almost wanted to catch the rail and swing back on again as the next pair of car steps flung by her.

Then a voice that sounded a little like Jane's said pleasantly in her ear: "Is this Lizzie Hope?" and Betty turned with a thrill of actual fright to face Nellie Carson and her little sister Emily.

"Bobbie'll be here in a minute to carry your suitcase," said Nellie efficiently; "he just went over to see if he could borrow Jake Peter's wheelbarrow in case you had a trunk. You didn't bring your trunk? O, but you're going to stay, aren't you? I'm goin' up to the city to take a p'sition, and Mother'd be awful lonesome. Sometime of course we'll send fer them to come, but now the children's little an' the country's better fer them. They gotta go to school awhile. You'll stay, won't you?"

"How do you know you'll want me?" laughed Betty, at her ease in this unexpected air of welcome.

"Why, of course we'd want you. Jane sent you. Jane wouldn't of sent you if you hadn't been a good scout. Jane knows. Besides, I've got two eyes, haven't I? I guess I can tell right off."

Emily's shy little hand stole into Betty's and the little girl looked up:

"I'm awful glad you come! I think you're awful pretty!"

"Thank you," said Betty, warmly squeezing the little confiding hand. It was the first time in her life that a little child had come close to her in this confiding way. Her life had not been among children.

Then Bob whirled up, bareheaded, freckled, whistling, efficient, and about twelve years old. He grabbed the suitcase, eyed the stranger with a pleasant grin, and stamped off into the darkness ahead of them.

It was a new experience to Betty to be walking down a village street with little houses on each side and lights and warmth and heads bobbing through the windows. It stirred some memory of long ago, before she could scarcely remember. She wondered, had her own mother ever lived in a small village?

"That's our church," confided Emily, as they passed a large frame building with pointed steeple and belfry. "They're goin' to have a entertainment t'morra night, an' we're all goin' and Ma said you cud go too."

"Isn't that lovely!" said Betty, feeling a sudden lump like tears in her throat. It was just like living out a fairy story. She hadn't expected to be taken right into family life this way.

"But how did you know I was coming on that train?" she asked the older girl suddenly. "Jane said she was going to telegraph, but I expected to have to hunt around to find the house."

"Oh, we just came down to every train after the telegram came. This is the last train tonight, and we were awful

scared for fear you wouldn't come till morning, an' have to
stay on the train all night. Ma says it isn't nice for a girl to
have to travel alone at night. Ma always makes Jane and me
go daytimes."

"It was just lovely of you," said Betty, wondering if she
was talking "natural" enough to please Jane.

"Did you bob your hair 'cause you had a fever?" asked
Nellie enviously.

"No," said Betty, "that is, I haven't been very well, and I
thought it might be good for me," she finished, wondering
how many questions like that it was going to be hard for her
to answer without telling a lie. A lie was something that her
father had made her feel would hurt him more deeply than
anything else she could do.

"I just love it," said Nellie enthusiastically. "I wanted to
cut mine, an' so did Jane, but Ma wouldn't let us. She says
God gave us our hair, an' we oughtta take care of it."

"That's true, too," said Betty. "I never thought about that.
But I guess mine will grow again after awhile. I think it will
be less trouble this way. But it's very dirty with traveling. I
think I'll have to wash it before I put it on a pillow."

That had troubled Betty greatly. She didn't know how to
get rid of that hair dye before Jane's family got used to having it dark.

"Sure, you can wash it, if you ain't 'fraid of takin' cold.
There's lots of hot water. Ma thought you'd maybe want to
take a bath. We've got a big tin bathtub out in the back
shed. Ma bought it off the Joneses when they got their porcelain one put into their house. We don't have no runnin'
water but we have an awful good well. Here's our house. I
guess Bob's got there first. See, Ma's out on the steps waitin'
fer us."

The house was a square wooden affair, long wanting
paint, and trimmed with little scrollwork around the diminutive front porch. The color was indescribable, blending
well into the surroundings either day or night. It had a
cheerful, decent look, but was very tiny. There was a small
yard about it with a picket fence, and a leafless lilac bush. A
cheerful barberry bush flanked the gate on either side. The

front door was open into a tiny hall and beyond the light streamed forth from a glass lamp set on a pleasant dining room table covered with a red cloth. Betty stepped inside the gate and found herself enveloped in two motherly arms, and then led into the light and warmth of the family dining room.

Chapter 8

There was a kettle of stew on the stove in the kitchen, kept hot from supper, for Betty, with fresh dumplings just mixed before the train came in, and bread and butter with applesauce and cookies. They made her sit right down and eat, before she even took her hat off, and they all sat around her and talked while she ate. It made her feel very much at home as if somehow she was a real relative.

It came over her once how different all this was from the house which she had called home all her life. The fine napery, the cut glass and silver, the stately butler! And here was she eating off a stone china plate thick enough for a table top, with a steel knife and fork and a spoon with the silver worn off the bowl. She could not help wondering what her stepmother would have said to the red and white tablecloth, and the green shades at the windows. There was an old sofa covered with carpet in the room with a flannel patchwork pillow, and a cat cuddled up cosily beside it purring away like a teakettle boiling. Somehow, poor as it was, it seemed infinitely more attractive than any room she had ever seen before, and she was charmed with the whole family. Bobbie sat at the other end of the table with his elbows on the table and his round eyes on her. When she smiled at him he winked one eye and grinned and then wriggled down under the table out of sight.

The mother had tired kind eyes and a firm cheerful mouth like Jane's. She took Betty right in as if she had been her sister's child.

"Come, now, get back there, Emily. Don't hang on Lizzie. She'll be tired to death of you right at the start. Give her a little peace while she eats her supper. How long have you and Jane been friends, Lizzie?" she asked, eager for news of her own daughter.

Betty's cheeks flushed and her eyes grew troubled. She was very much afraid that being Lizzie was going to be hard work:

"Why, not so very long," she said hesitatingly.

"Are you one of the girls in her factory?"

"Oh, no!" said Betty wildly, wondering what would come next. "We—just met—that is—why—*out one evening!*" she finished desperately.

"Oh, I see!" said the mother. "Yes, she wrote about going out sometimes, mostly to the movies. And to church. My children always make it a point to go to church wherever they are. I brought 'em up that way. I hope you go to church."

"I shall love to," said Betty eagerly.

"Is your mother living?" was the next question.

"No," answered Betty. "Mother and Father are both dead and I've been having rather a hard time. Jane was kind to me when I was in trouble."

"I'll warrant you! That's Jane!" beamed her mother happily. "Jane always was a good girl, if I do say so. I knew Jane was at her tricks again when she sent me that telegram."

"Ma's got you a place already!" burst out Nellie eagerly.

"Now, Nellie, you said you'd let Ma tell that!" reproached Bob. "You never can keep your mouth shut."

"There! There! Bob, don't spoil the evening with anything unkind," warned the mother. "Yes, Lizzie, I got you a position. It just happened I had the chance, and I took it, though I don't really b'lieve that anythin' in this world just happens, of course. But it did seem providential. Mrs. Hathaway wanted somebody to look after her little girl. She's only three years old and she is possessed to run away every chance she gets. Course I s'pose she's spoiled. Most rich children are. Now, my children wouldn't have run away. They always thought too much of what I said to make me trouble. But that's neither here nor there. She does it, and besides her ma is an invalid. She had an operation, so she has to lie still a good bit, and can't be bothered. She wants somebody just to take the little girl out walking and keep her happy in the house, an' all."

"How lovely!" exclaimed Betty. "I shall enjoy it, I know."

"She's awful pretty!" declared Emily eagerly. "Got gold curls and blue eyes just like you, and she has ever an' ever so many little dresses, and wears pink shoes and blue shoes, an' rides a tricycle."

"How interesting!" said Betty.

"You'll get good wages," said the mother. "She said she'd give you six dollars a week, an' mebbe more, an' you'd get some of your meals."

"Then I can pay my board to you," cried Betty.

"Don't worry about that, child. We'll fix that up somehow. We're awful glad to have you come, and I guess we shall like each other real well. Now, children, it's awful late. Get to bed. Scat! Lizzie can have her bath an' get to bed, too. Come mornin's half way here already!"

The children said good-night and Betty was introduced to the tin bathtub and improvised bathroom—a neat little addition to the kitchen evidently intended originally for a laundry. She wanted to laugh when she saw the primitive makeshifts, but instead the tears came into her eyes to think how many luxuries she had taken all her life as a matter of course and never realized how hard it was for people who had none. In fact it had never really entered her head before that there were people who had no bathrooms.

Betty was not exactly accustomed to washing her own hair, and with the added problem of the dye it was quite a task; but she managed it at last, using all the hot water, to get it so that the rinsing water was clear, and her hair felt soft. Then, attired in the same warm nightgown she had worn the night before, which Jane had thoughtfully put in the suitcase—otherwise filled with old garments she wished to send home—Betty pattered upstairs to the little room with the sloping roof and the dormer window and crept into bed with Nellie. That young woman had purposely stayed awake, and kept Betty as long as she could talk, telling all the wonderful things she wanted to know about city life, and Betty found herself in deep water sometimes because the city life she knew about was so very different from the city life that Jane would know. But at last sleep won, and Nellie had to give up because her last question was answered with silence. The guest was deep in slumber.

The next morning the children took her over the house, out in the yard, showing her everything. Then they had to take her down to the village and explain all about the little town and its people. They were crazy about Betty's beautiful hair and much disappointed when she would insist on wearing her hat. It was a bright sunny morning, not very cold, and they told her that nobody wore a hat except to church or to go on the train, but Betty had a feeling that her hair might attract attention, and in her first waking hours a great shadow of horror had settled upon her when she realized that her people would leave no stone unturned to find her. It was most important that she should do or be nothing whereby she might be recognized. She even thought of getting a cap and apron to wear when attending her small charge, but Nellie told her they didn't do that in the country and she would be thought stuck-up, so she desisted. But she drew the blue serge skirt up as high above her waistband as possible when she dressed in the morning so that she might look like a little girl and no one would suspect her of being a runaway bride. Also she had a consultation with herself in the small hours of the morning while Nellie was still fast asleep, and settled with her conscience just what she would tell about her past and what she would keep to herself. There was a certain reserve that anyone might have, and if she was frank about a few facts no one would be likely to question further.

So next morning she told Mrs. Carson that since her parents' death she had lived with a woman who knew her father well, but lately things had been growing very unpleasant and she found she had to leave. She had left under such conditions that she could not bring away anything that belonged to her, so she would have to work and earn some more clothes.

Mrs. Carson looked into her sweet eyes and agreed that it was the best thing she could do; they might follow her up and make all sorts of trouble for her in her new home if she wrote for her things; and so the matter dropped. They were simple folks, who took things at their face value and were not over inquisitive.

On the third day there arrived a long letter from Jane in which she gave certain suggestions concerning the new member of the family, and ended: "Ma, she's got a story, but don't make her tell any more of it than she wants. She's awful sensitive about it, and trust me, she's all right! She's been through a lot. Just make her feel she's got some folks that loves and trusts her."

Ma, wise beyond her generation and experience, said no more, and took the little new daughter into her heart. She took the opportunity to inform the village gossips that a friend of Jane's had come to rest up and get a year's country air, boarding with them; and so the amalgamation of Betty Stanhope into the life of the little town began.

The "job" proved to be for only part of the day, so that Betty was free most of the mornings to help around the house and take almost a daughter's place. That she was a rare girl is proved by the way she entered into her new life. It was almost as if she had been born again, and entered into a new universe, so widely was her path diverging from everything which had been familiar in the old life. So deep had been her distress before she came into it that this new existence, despite its hard and unaccustomed work, seemed almost like heaven.

It is true there was much bad grammar and slang, but that did not trouble Betty. She had been brought up to speak correctly, and it was second nature to her, but no one had ever drummed it into her what a crime against culture an illiterate way of speaking could be. She never got into the way of speaking that way herself, but it seemed a part of these people she had come to know and admire so thoroughly, as much as for a rose to have thorns, and so she did not mind it. Her other world had been so all wrong for years that the hardships of this one were nothing. She watched them patch and sacrifice cheerfully to buy their few little plain coarse new things. She marveled at their sweetness and content, where those of her world would have thought they could not exist under the circumstances.

She learned to make that good stew with carrots and celery and parsley and potatoes and the smallest possible amount of meat, that had tasted so delicious the night she arrived. She learned the charms of the common little bean, and was proud indeed the day she set upon the table a luscious pan of beans of her own baking, rich and sweet and brown with their coating of molasses well baked through them. She even learned to make bread and never let anyone guess that she had always supposed it something mysterious.

During the week that Nellie was preparing to go to the city, Betty had lessons in sewing. Nellie would bring down an old garment, so faded and worn that it would seem only fit for the ragbag. She would rip and wash, dye with a mysterious little package of stuff, press, and behold, there would come forth pretty breadths of cloth, blue or brown or green, or whatever color was desired. It seemed like magic. And then a box of paper patterns would be brought out, and the whole evening would be spent in contriving how to get out a dress, with the help of trimmings or sleeves of another material. Betty would watch and gradually try to help, but she found there were so many strange things to be considered. There, for instance, was the up and down of a thing and the right and wrong of it. It was exactly like life. And one had to plan not to have both sleeves for one arm, and to have the nap of the goods running down always. It was as complicated as learning a new language. But at the end of the week there came forth two pretty dresses and a blouse. Betty, as she sat sewing plain seams and trying to help all she could, kept thinking of the many beautiful frocks she had thrown aside in the years gone by, and of the rich store of pretty things that she had left when she fled. If only Nellie and Jane and little Emily could have them! Ah, and if only she herself might have them now! How she needed them! For a girl who had always had all she wanted it was a great change to get along with this one coarse serge and aprons.

But the sewing and other work had not occupied them so fully that they had not had time to introduce Betty into their little world. The very next evening after she arrived she had been taken to that wonderful church entertainment that the girls had told her about on the way from the station, and there she had met the minister's wife and been invited to her Sabbath school class.

Betty would not have thought of going if Nellie and her mother had not insisted. In fact, she shrank unspeakably from going out into the little village world. But it was plain that this was expected of her, and if she remained here she must do as they wanted her to do. It was the least return she could make to these kind people.

The question of whether or not she should remain began to come to her insistently now. The children clamored every day for her to bind herself for the winter, and Jane's mother had made her most welcome. She saw that they really wanted her; why should she not stay? And yet it did seem queer to arrange deliberately to spend a whole year in a poor uncultured family. Still, where could she go and hope to remain unknown if she attempted to get back into her own class? It was impossible. Her mother had just the one elderly cousin whom she had always secretly looked to to help her in any time of need, but his failing her and sending that telegram without even a good wish in it, just at the last minute, too, made her feel it was of no use to appeal to him. Besides, that was the first place her stepmother would seek for her. She had many good society friends, but none who would stand by her in trouble. No one with whom she had ever been intimate enough to confide in. She had been kept strangely alone in her little world after all, hedged in by servants everywhere. And now that she was suddenly on her own responsibility, she felt a great timidity in taking any step alone. Sometimes at night when she thought what she had done she was so frightened that her heart would beat wildly as if she were running away from them all yet. It was like a nightmare that pursued her.

Mrs. Hathaway had sent for her and made arrangements for her to begin her work with the little Elise the following week when the present governess should leave, and Betty felt that this might prove a very pleasant way to earn her living. The Hathaways lived in a great brick house away back from the street in grounds that occupied what in the city would have been a whole block. There was a high hedge about the place so that one could not see the road, and there were flower beds, a great fountain, and a rustic summerhouse. Betty did not see why days passed in such a pleasant place would not be delightful in summertime. She was not altogether sure whether she would like to have to be a sort of servant in the house—and of course these cold fall days she would have to be much in the house—but the nursery had a big fireplace in it, a long chest under the window where toys were kept, and many comfortable chairs. That ought to be pleasant, too. Besides, she was not just out looking for pleasant things on this trip. She was trying to get away from unbearable ones, and she ought to be very thankful indeed to have fallen on such comfort as she had.

There was another element in the Carson home that drew her strongly, although she was shy about even thinking of it, and that was the frank, outspoken Christianity. "Ma" tempered all her talk with it, adjusted all her life to God and what He would think about her actions, spoke constantly of what was right and wrong. Betty had never lived in an atmosphere where right and wrong mattered. Something sweet and pure like an instinct in her own soul had held her always from many of the ways of those about her, perhaps the spirit of her sweet mother allowed to be one of those who "bear them up, lest at any time they dash their feet against a stone." Or it might have been some memory of the teachings of her father, whom she adored, and who in his last days often talked with her alone about how he and her own mother would want her to live. But now, safe and quiet in this shelter of a real home, poor though it was, the God-instinct stirred within her, caused her to wonder what He was, why she was alive, and if He cared? One could not live with Mrs. Carson without thinking something about her God, for He was an ever-present help in all her times of need, and she never hesitated to give God the glory for all she had achieved, and for all the blessings she had received.

The very first Sabbath in the little white church stirred still deeper her awakening interest in spiritual things. The minister's wife was a sweet-faced woman who called her "my dear" and invited her to come and see her, and when she began to teach the lesson Betty found to her amazement that it was interesting. She spoke of God in much the same familiar way that "Ma" had done, only with a gentler refinement, and made the girls very sure that whatever anybody else believed, Mrs. Thornley was a very intimate friend of Jesus Christ. Betty loved her at once, but so shy was she that the minister's wife never dreamed it, and remarked to her husband Sunday night after church, when they were having their little quiet Sabbath talk together, that she was afraid she was going to have a hard time winning that little new girl that had come to live with Mrs. Carson.

"Somehow I can't get away from the thought that she comes from aristocracy somewhere," she added. "It's the way she turns her head, or lifts her eyes or the quiet assurance with which she answers. And she smiles, Charles, never grins like the rest. She is delicious, but somehow I find myself wondering if I have remembered to black my shoes and whether my hat is on straight, when she looks at me."

"Well, maybe she's the daughter of some black sheep who has gone down a peg, and our Father has sent her here for you to help her back again," said her husband with an adorable look at his helper. "If anyone can do it you can."

"I'm not so sure," she said, shaking her head. "She maybe doesn't need me. She has Mrs. Carson, remember, and she is a host in herself. If anybody can lead her to Christ she can, plain as she is."

"Undoubtedly you were meant to help, too, dear, or she would not have been sent to you."

His wife smiled brilliantly a look of thorough understanding: "Oh, I know. I'm not going to shirk any but I wish I knew more about her. She is so sad and quiet, I can't seem to get at her."

Even at that moment Betty lay in her little cot bed under the roof thinking about the minister's wife and what she had said about Christ being always near, ready to show what to do, if one had the listening heart and the ready spirit. Would Christ tell her what to do, she wondered, now right here, if she were to ask Him? Would He show her whether to stay in this place or seek further to hide herself from the world? Would He show her how to earn her living and make her life right and sweet as it ought to be?

Then she closed her eyes and whispered softly under the sheltering bedclothes. "O Christ, if You are here, please show me somehow and teach me to understand."

Chapter 9

When Betty had been in Tinsdale about a month it was discovered that she could play the piano. It happened on a rainy Sunday in Sunday school, and the regular pianist was late. The superintendent looked about helplessly and asked if there was anybody present who could play, although he knew the musical ability of everybody in the village. The minister's wife had already pleaded a cut finger which was well wrapped up in a bandage, and he was about to ask someone to start the tune without the piano when Mrs. Thornton leaned over with a sudden inspiration to Betty and asked:

"My dear, you couldn't play for us, could you?"

Betty smiled assent, and without any ado went to the instrument, not realizing until after she had done so that it would have been better policy for her to have remained as much in the background as possible, and not to have shown any accomplishments lest people should suspect her position. However, she was too new at acting a part to always think of these little things, and she played the hymns so well that they gathered about her after the hour was over and openly rejoiced that there was another pianist in town. The leader of Christian Endeavor asked her to play in their meeting sometimes, and Betty found herself quite popular. The tallest girl in their class, who had not noticed her before, smiled at her and patronized her after she came back

from playing the first hymn, and asked her where she
learned to play so well.

"Oh, I used to take lessons before my father died," she
said, realizing that she must be careful.

Emily and Bob came home in high feather and told their
mother, who had not been able to get out that morning, and
she beamed on Betty with as warm a smile as if she had
been her own daughter.

"Now, ain't that great!" she said, and her voice sounded
boyish just like Jane's. "Why, we'll have to get a pianna. I
heard you could get 'em cheap in the cities sometimes—
old-fashioned ones, you know. I heard they have so many
old-fashioned ones that they have to burn 'em to get rid of
'em, and they even give 'em away sometimes. I wonder,
could we find out and get hold of one?"

"I guess 'twould cost too much to get it here," said Bob
practically. "My! I wisht we had one. Say, Lizzie, 'f we had a
pianna would you show me how to read notes?"

"Of course," said Betty.

"Well, we'll get one somehow! We always do when we
need anything awfully. Look at the bathtub! Good-night!
I'm goin' to earn one myself!" declared Bob.

"Mrs. Crosby's gotta get a new one. P'raps she'll sell us
her old one cheap."

That was the way the music idea started, and nothing else
was talked of at the table for days but how to get a piano.
Then one day Emily came rushing home from school all out
of breath, her eyes as bright as stars, and her cheeks like
roses. "Mrs. Barlow came to our school today and talked to
the teacher, and I heard her say she was going away for the
winter. She's going to store her goods in the service company barn, but she wants to get somebody to take care of
her piano. I stepped right up and told her my mother was
looking for a piano, and we'd be real careful of it, and she's
just delighted; and—it's coming tomorrow morning at nine
o'clock! The man's going to bring it!"

She gasped it out so incoherently that they had to make
her tell it over twice to get any sense out of it; but when Bob

finally understood he caught his little sister in his arms and
hugged her with a big smacking kiss.

"You sure are a little peach, Em'ly!" he shouted. "You're a
pippin of the pippins! I didn't know you had that much
nerve, you kid, you! I sure am proud of you! My! Think of
havin' a pianna! Say, Lizzie, I can play the base of chopsticks
now!"

The next evening when Betty got home from the
Hathaways there was the piano standing in the big space
opposite the windows in the dining room. Ma had elected
to have it there rather than in the front room, because it
might often be too cold in the front room for the children to
practice, and besides it wouldn't be good for the piano. So
the piano became a beloved member of the family, and
Betty began to give instructions in music, wondering at herself that she knew how, for her own music had been most
desultory, and nobody had ever cared whether she practiced or not. She had been allowed to ramble among the
great masters for the most part unconducted, with the mea-
gerest technique, and her own interpretation. She could
read well and her sense of time and rhythm were natural,
else she would have made worse work of it than she did. But
she forthwith set herself to practicing, realizing that it
might yet stand her in good stead since she had to earn her
living.

Little Emily and Bob stood one on either side and
watched her as she played, with wondering admiration, and
when Betty went to help their mother Bob would sit down
and try to imitate what she had done. Failing, he would fall
headlong into the inevitable chopsticks, beating it out with
the air of a master.

It was the piano that brought to Betty's realization the
first real meaning of the Sabbath day. Bob came down early
and went at the piano as usual, banging out chopsticks, and
a one-fingered arrangement of "The Long, Long Trail,"
while his mother was getting breakfast. Betty was making
the coffee, proud of the fact that she had learned how. But
Bob had accomplished only a brief hint of his regular program when the music stopped suddenly and Betty glanced

through the kitchen door to see Ma standing with her hand on her son's shoulder and a look on her face she had not seen before: It was quite gentle, but it was decided.

"No, Bob! We won't have that kinda music on Sunday," she said. "This is God's day, an' we'll have all we can rightly do to keep it holy without luggin' in weekday music to make us forget it. You just get t' work an' learn 'Safely Through Another Week,' and if you can't play it right you get Lizzie to teach you."

Bob pouted:

"There ain't nothing' wrong with chopsticks, Ma. 'Tain't got words to it."

"Don't make any difference. It b'longs to weekdays an' fun, an' anyhow it makes you think of other things, an' you can't keep your mind on God. That's what Sunday was made fer, to kinda tone us up to God, so's we won't get so far away in the week that we won't be any kind of ready for heaven sometime. An' anyhow, 'tisn't seemly. You better go learn your Golden Text, Bob. The minister'll be disappointed if you don't have it fine."

Betty stood by the window thoughtfully looking out. Was that what Sunday was made for, or was it only a quaint idea of this original woman? She wished she knew. Perhaps sometime she would know the minister's wife well enough to ask. She would have liked to ask Ma more about it, but somehow felt shy. But Ma herself was started now, and when she came back to the kitchen, as if she felt some explanation was due the new inmate of the family, she said:

"I don't know how you feel about it. I know city folks don't always hold to the old ways. But it always seemed to me God meant us to stick to Sunday, and make it diff'rent from other days. I never would let my children go visitin', nor play ball, an' we always tried to have something good for supper fixed the night before. I heard somebody say a long time ago that it says somewhere in the Bible that Sunday was meant to be a sign forever between God and folks. The ones that keeps it are His'n, an' them as don't aren't. Anyhow, that's the only day we have got to kinda find out what's wanted of us. You wouldn't mind just playin' hymns and Sunday things t'day, would you?"

"Oh, no," said Betty interested. "I like it. It sounds so kind of safe, and as if God cared. I never thought much about it before. You think God really thinks about us and knows what we're doing then, don't you?"

"Why, sure, child. I don't just think, I *know* He does. Hadn't you never got onto that? Why, you poor little ducky, you! O' course He does."

"I'd like to feel sure that He was looking out for me," breathed Betty wistfully.

"Well, you can!" said Ma, hurrying back to see that her bacon didn't burn. "It's easy as rollin' off a log."

"What would I have to do?"

"Why, just b'lieve."

"Believe?" asked Betty utterly puzzled. "Believe what?"

"Why, believe that He'll do it. He said 'Come unto me, an' I will give you rest,' an' He said, 'Cast your burden on the Lord,' an' He said 'Castin' all yer care 'pon Him, fer He careth fer you,' an' a whole lot more such things, an' you just got to take it fer straight, an' act to it."

"But how could I?" asked Betty.

"Just run right up to your room now, while you're feelin' that way, an' kneel down by your bed an' tell Him what you just told me," said Mrs. Carson, stirring the fried potatoes with her knife to keep them from burning. "It won't take you long, an' I'll tend the coffee. Just you tell Him you want Him to take care of you, an' you'll believe what I told you He said. It's all in the Bible, an' you can read it for yourself, but I wouldn't take the time now. Just run along an' speak it out with Him, and, then come down to breakfast."

Betty was standing by the kitchen door, her hand on her heart, as if about to do some great wonderful thing that frightened her:

"But, Mrs. Carson, suppose, maybe, He might not be pleased with me. Suppose I've done something that He doesn't like, something that makes Him ashamed of me."

"Oh, why, didn't you know He fixed for all that when He sent His Son to be the Saviour of the world? We all do wrong things, an' everybody has sinned. But ef we're rightly sorry, he'll forgive us, and make us His children."

Betty suddenly sat down in a chair near the door:

"But, Mrs. Carson, I'm not sure I *am* sorry—at least I know I'm *not*. I'm afraid I'd do it all over again if I got in the same situation."

Mrs. Carson stood back from the stove and surveyed her thoughtfully a moment:

"Well, then, like's not it wasn't wrong at all, and if it wasn't He ain't displeased. You can bank on that. You better go talk it out to Him. Just get it off your mind. I'll hold up breakfast a minute while you roll it on Him and, depend on it, He'll show you in plenty of time for the next move."

Betty with her cheeks very red and her eyes shining went up to her little cot, and with locked door knelt and tried to talk to God for the first time in her life. It seemed queer to her, but when she arose and hurried back to her duties she had sense of having a real Friend who knew all about her and could look after things a great deal better than she could.

That night she went with Bob and Emily to the young people's meeting and heard them talk about Christ familiarly as if they knew Him. It was all strange and new and wonderful to Betty, and she sat listening and wondering. The old question of whether she was pleasing her earthly father was merging itself into the desire to please her heavenly Father.

There were of course many hard and unpleasant things about her new life. There were so many things to learn, and she was so awkward at work of all kinds! Her hands seemed so small and inadequate when she tried to wring clothes or scrub a dirty step. Then, too, her young charge, Elise Hathaway, was spoiled and hard to please, and she was daily tried by the necessity of inventing ways of discipline for the poor little neglected girl which yet would not bring down a protest from her even more undisciplined mother. If she had been independent she would not have remained with Mrs. Hathaway, for sometimes the child was unbearable in her naughty tantrums, and it took all her nerve and strength to control her. She would come back to the little gray house too weary even to smile, and the keen eye of Ma would look at her wisely and wonder if something ought not to be done about it.

Betty felt that she must keep this place, of course, because it was necessary for her to be able to pay some board. She could not be beholden to the Carsons. And they had been so kind, and were teaching her so many things, that it seemed the best and safest place she could be in. So the days settled down into weeks, and a pleasant life grew up about her, so different from the old one that more and more the hallucination was with her that she had become another creature, and the old life had gone out forever.

Of course as striking looking a girl as Betty could not enter into the life of a little town even as humbly as through the Carson home, without causing some comment and speculation. People began to notice her. The church ladies looked after her and remarked on her hair, her complexion, and her graceful carriage, and some shook their heads and said they should think Mrs. Hathaway would want to know a little more about her before she put her only child in her entire charge; and they told weird stories about girls they had known or heard of.

Down at the firehouse, which was the real clearinghouse of Tinsdale for all the gossip that came along and went the rounds, they took up the matter in full session several evenings in succession. Some of the younger members made crude remarks about Betty's looks, and some of the older ones allowed that she was entirely too pretty to be without a history. They took great liberties with their surmises. The only two, the youngest of them all, who might have defended her, had been unconsciously snubbed by her when they tried to be what Bobbie called "fresh" with her, and so she was at their mercy. But if she had known it she probably would have been little distubed. They seemed so far removed from her two worlds, so utterly apart from herself. It would not have occurred to her that they could do her any harm.

One night the firehouse gang had all assembled save one, a little shrimp of a good-for-nothing, nearly hairless, toothless, cunning-eyed, and given to drink when he could lay lips on any. He had a wide loose mouth with a tendency to droop crookedly, and his hands were always clammy and limp. He ordinarily sat tilted back against the wall to the right of the engine, sucking an old clay pipe. He had a way of often turning the conversation to imply some deep mystery known only to himself behind the life of almost anyone discussed. He often added choice embellishments to whatever tale went forth as authentic to go the rounds of the village, and he acted the part of a collector of themes and details for the evening conversations.

His name was Abijah Gage.

"Bi not come yet?" asked the fire chief settling a straw comfortably between his teeth and looking around on the group. "Must be somepin' doin'. Don't know when Bi's been away."

"He went up to town this mornin' early," volunteered Dunc Withers. "Reckon he was thirsty. Guess he'll be back on the evenin' train. That's her comin' in now."

"Bars all closed in the city," chuckled the chief. "Won't get much comfort there."

"You bet Bi knows some place to get it. He won't come home thirsty, that's sure."

"I dunno, they say the lid's down pretty tight."

"Aw, shucks!" sneered Dunc. "Bet I could get all I wanted."

Just then the door opened and Abijah Gage walked in, with a toothless grin all around.

"Hello, Bi, get tanked up, did yeh?" greeted the chief.

"Well, naow, an' ef I did, what's that to you?" responded Bi, slapping the chief's broad shoulder with a folded newspaper he carried. "You don't 'spose I'm goin' to tell, an' get my frien's in trouble?"

"Le's see yer paper, Bi," said Dunc, snatching at it as Bi passed to his regular seat.

Bi surrendered his paper with the air of one granting a high favor and sank to his chair and his pipe.

"How's crops in the city?" asked Hank Fielder, and Bi's tale was set a-going. Bi could talk; that was one thing that always made him welcome.

Dunc was deep in the paper. Presently he turned it over:

"Whew!" he said speculatively. "If that don't look like that little lollypop over to Carson's I'll eat my hat! What's her name?"

They all drew around the paper and leaned over Dunc's shoulder squinting at the picture, all but Bi, who was lighting his pipe:

"They're as like as two peas!" said one.

"It sure must be her sister!" declared another.

"Don't see no resemblance 'tall," declared the chief, flinging back to his comfortable chair. "She's got short hair, an' she's only a kid. This one's growed up!"

"She might a cut her hair," suggested one.

Bi pricked up his ears, narrowed his cunning eyes, and slouched over to the paper, looking at the picture keenly:

"Read it out, Dunc!" he commanded.

"Five thousand dollars reward for information concerning Elizabeth Stanhope!"

There followed a description in detail of her size, height, coloring, and so forth.

An inscrutable look overspread Bi's face and hid the cunning in his eyes. He slouched to his seat during the reading and tilted back comfortably smoking, but he narrowed his eyes to a slit and spoke little during the remainder of the evening. They discussed the picture and the possibility of the girl in the paper being a relative of the girl at Carson's, but as Bi did not come forward with information the subject languished. Someone said he had heard the Carson kid call her Lizzie, he thought, but he wasn't sure. Ordinarily Bi would have known the full name, but Bi seemed to be dozing, and so the matter was finally dropped. But the hounds were out and on the scent, and it was well for Betty sleeping quietly in her little cot beneath the roof of the humble Carson home, that she had committed her all to her heavenly Father before she slept.

Chapter 10

"Well, he gave me notice t'day," said James Ryan sadly as Jane and he rounded the corner from her boardinghouse and turned toward their favorite movie theater. "I been expectin' it, an' now it's come!"

Jane stopped short on the sidewalk appalled:

"He gave you notice!" she exclaimed, as if she could not believe it was true. "Now, Jimmie! You don't mean it? Did he find any fault? He'd better not? B'leeve me, if he did he gets a piece of *my* mind, even if I am a poor workin' girl!"

"Oh, no, he didn't find any fault," said Jimmie cheerfully. "He was awful nice! He said he'd recommend me away up high. He's gonta give me time everyday to hunt a new place, an' he's gonta recommend me to some of his rich friends."

"But what's the matter of him keepin' you? Did you ast him that?"

"Oh, he told me right out that things wasn't working the way he hoped when he started; the war and all had upset his prospects, and he couldn't afford to keep me. He's gonta take an office way downtown and do his own letters. He says if he ever succeeds in business and I'm free to come to him he'll take me back. Oh, he's pleased with me all right! He's a peach! He certainly is."

"Jimmie, what d'you tell him?"

"Tell him? There wasn't much for me to tell him, only I was sorry, and I thanked him, and I told him I was gonta stick by him as long as I didn't have a place. Oh course I can't live on air, but seeing he's willing I should go out and hunt a place every day, why I ain't that mean that I can't write a few letters for him now and then. He don't have that many, and it keeps me in practice. I s'pose I've got to get another place but I haven't tried yet. I can't somehow bring myself to give him up. I kind of wanted to stick in my first place a long time. It doesn't look well to be changing."

"Well, if it ain't your fault, you know, why you can't help it," advised Jane.

They were seated in the theater by this time, and the screen claimed their attention. It was just at the end of the funny reel, and both forgot more serious matters in following the adventures of a dog and a bear who were chasing each other through endless halls and rooms, to say nothing of bathtubs, and wash boilers, and dining tables, and anything that came in their way, with a shock to the people who happened to be around when they passed. But suddenly the film ended and the announcements for the next week began to flash on the screen.

"We must go to that, sure!" said Jimmie, nudging Jane, as the Mary Pickford announcement was put on.

Then immediately afterward came the photograph of a beautiful girl, and underneath in great letters:

FIVE THOUSAND DOLLARS' REWARD FOR
ACCURATE INFORMATION AS TO THE
PRESENT WHEREABOUTS OF
ELIZABETH STANHOPE

There followed further particulars and an address and the showing stayed on the screen for a full minute.

Jane sat gripping the arms of the seat and trying to still the wild excitement that possessed her, while her eyes looked straight into the eyes of the little bride whom she had helped to escape on the night of her wedding.

Jimmie took out his pencil and wrote down the address in shorthand, but Jane did not notice. She was busy thinking what she ought to do.

"What do you s'pose they want her for?" she asked in a breathless whisper, as a new feature film began to dawn on the screen.

"Oh, she's mebbe eloped," said the wise young man, "or there might be some trouble about property. There mostly is."

Jane said no more, and the pictures began again, but her mind was not following them. She was very quiet on the way home, and when Jimmie asked her if she had a grouch on she shivered and said, no, she guessed she was tired. Then she suddenly asked him what time he was going out to hunt for another job. He told her he couldn't be sure. He would call her up about noon and let her know. Could she manage to get out awhile and meet him? She wasn't sure either, but would see when he called her up. And so they parted for the night.

The next morning when Reyburn entered his office Jimmie was already seated at his typewriter. On Reyburn's desk lay a neatly typed copy of the announcement that had been put on the screen the night before.

"What's this, Ryan?" he questioned as he took his seat and drew the paper toward him.

"Something I saw last night on the screen at the movies, sir. I thought it might be of interest."

"Were you thinking of trying for the reward?" asked Reyburn with a comical smile. "What is it, anyway?" And he began to read.

"Oh, no sir!" said Jimmie. "*I* couldn't, of course; but I thought mebbe *you'd* be able to find out something about her and get all that money. That would help you through until you got started in your own business."

"H'm! That's kind of you, Ryan," said the young lawyer, reading the paper with a troubled frown. "I'm afraid it's hardly in my line, however. I'm not a detective, you know." He laid the paper down and looked thoughtfully out of the window.

"Oh, of course not, sir!" Jimmie hastened to apologize. "Only you know a lot of society folks in the city, and I thought you might think of some way of finding out where she is. I know it isn't up to what you ought to be doing, sir, but it wouldn't do any harm. You could work it through me, you know, and nobody need ever know 'twas you got the reward. I'd be glad to help you out doing all I could, but of course it would take your brains to get the information, sir. You see, it would be to my interest, because then you could afford to keep me, and—I like you, Mr. Reyburn, I certainly do. I would hate to leave you."

"Well, now, I appreciate that, Ryan. It's very thoughtful of you. I scarcely think there would be any possibility of my finding out anything about this girl, but I certainly appreciate your thoughtfulness. I'll make a note of it, and if anything turns up I'll let you know. I don't believe, however, that I would care to go after a reward even through someone else. You know, I was at that wedding, Ryan!" His eyes were dreamily watching the smoke from a distant funnel over the rooftops in line with his desk.

"You were!" said Jimmie, watching his employer with rapt admiration. He had no higher ambition than to look like Warren Reyburn and have an office of his own.

"Yes, I was there," said Reyburn again, but his tone was so far off that Jimmie dared approach no nearer, and resumed the letter he was typing.

About noon Jimmie called up the factory while Reyburn was out to lunch and told Jane that he expected to go out at two o'clock. Could she meet him and walk a little way with him? Jane said no, she couldn't, but she would try and see him the next day, then he could tell her how he had made out.

At exactly five minutes after two, Jane, having watched from a telephone booth in a drugstore—until Jimmie went by, hurried up to Reyburn's office and tapped on the door, her heart in her mouth lest he should be occupied with someone else and not be able to see her before her few minutes of leave which she had obtained from the factory should have expired.

Reyburn himself opened the door to her, and treated her as if she had been a lady every inch, handing her a chair and speaking quite as if she were attired in sealskin and diamonds.

She looked him over with bright eyes of approval. Jane was a born sentimentalist, fed on the movies. Not for anything would she have had a knight rescue her lady fair who did not look the part. She was entirely satisfied with this one. In fact, she was almost tongue-tied with admiration for the moment.

Then she rallied to the speech she had prepared:

"Mr. Reyburn," she said, "I came to see you about a matter of very great importance. I heard you was a great lawyer, and I've got a friend that's in trouble. I thought mebbe you could do something about it. But first, I want to ast you a question, an' I want you to consider it perfectly confidential!"

Jane took great credit to herself that she had assembled all these words and memorized them so perfectly.

"Certainly!" said Reyburn gravely, wondering what kind of a customer he had now.

"I don't want you to think I can't pay for it," said Jane, laying down a five-dollar bill grandly. "I know you can't afford to waste your valuable time even to answer a question."

"Oh, that's all right," said Reyburn heartily. "Let me hear what the question is first. There may be no charge."

"No," said Jane hastily, laying the bill firmly on the desk before him. "I shan't feel right astin' unless I know it's to be paid for."

"Oh, very well," said Reyburn, taking the bill and laying it to one side. "Now, what is the question?"

"Well, Mr. Reyburn, will you please tell me what would anybody want to offer a reward, a big reward, like a thousand dollars—or several of them—for information about anyone? Could you think of any reason?"

Reyburn started. Reward again! This was uncanny. Probably this girl had been to the movies and seen the same picture that Ryan had told him about. But he smiled gravely and answered, watching her quizzically the while:

"Well, they might love the person that had disappeared," he suggested at random.

"Oh, no!" said Jane decidedly. "They didn't! I know that fer a fac'! What else could it be?"

"Well, they might have a responsibility!" he said thoughtfully.

"No chance!" said Jane scornfully.

"Couldn't they be anxious, don't you think?"

"Not so's you'd notice it."

"Well, there might be some property to be divided, perhaps."

"I'd thought of that," said Jane, her face growing practical. "It would have to be a good deal of property to make them offer a big reward, wouldn't it?"

"I should think so," answered Reyburn politely, watching her plain eager face amusedly. He could not quite get at her idea in coming to him.

"Would her coming of age have anything to do with it?" put Jane, referring to a much folded paper she carried in her hand, as if she had a written catechism which she must go through.

"It might." Reyburn was growing interested. This queer visitor evidently had thought something out, and was being very cautious.

"I really can't answer very definitely without knowing more of the circumstances," he said with sudden alarm lest the girl might take some random answer and let serious matters hinge on his word.

"Well, there's just one more," she said, looking down at her paper. "If a man was trying to make a girl marry him when she just hated him, could anybody make her do it, and would anybody have a right to put her in an insane 'sylum or anythin' ef she wouldn't?"

"Why, no, of course not! Where did you ever get such a ridiculous idea?" He sat up suddenly, annoyed beyond expression over disturbing suggestions that seemed to rise like a bevy of black bats all around the borders of his mind.

"See here," he said, sitting up very straight. "I really can't answer any more blind questions. I've got to know what I'm talking about. Why, I may be saying the most impossible things without knowing it."

"I know," said Jane, looking at him gravely. "I've thought of that, but you've said just the things I thought you would. Well, say, if I tell you about it can you promise on yer honor you won't ever breathe a word of it? Not to nobody? Whether you take the case or not?"

"Why, certainly, you can trust me to look out for any confidence you may put in me. If you can't I should prefer that you say nothing more."

"Oh, I c'n trust you all right," said Jane smiling. "I just mean, would you be 'lowed to keep it under yer hat?"

"Would I be allowed? What do you mean?"

"I mean would the law let you? You wouldn't *have* to go an' tell where she was or nothin' an' give her away? You'd be 'lowed to keep it on the q.t. an' take care of her?"

"You mean would it be right and honorable for me to protect my client? Why, certainly."

"Well, I mean you wouldn't get into no trouble if you did."

"Of course not."

"Well, then I'll tell you."

Chapter 11

Jane opened a small shabby handbag, and took out a folded newspaper, opening it up and spreading it on the desk before him. "There!" she said, and then watched his face critically.

Reyburn looked, and found himself looking into Betty's eyes. Only a newspaper cut, and poor at that, but wonderfully real and mournful, as they had struck him when she lifted them for that swift glance before she sank in the church aisle.

"Where did you get this?" he asked, his voice suddenly husky.

"Out o' the mornin' paper." Her tone was low and excited. "Were you wanting to try for the reward?" Reyburn asked.

There was a covert sneer in the question from which the girl shrank perceptibly. She sprang to her feet, her eyes flashing:

"If that's what you take me for, I better be goin'!" she snapped and reached out her hand for the paper. But Reyburn's hand covered the paper, and his tone was respectful and apologetic as he said:

"Excuse me, I didn't quite understand, I see. Sit down, please. You and I must understand each other or there is no use in our talking. You can trust me to keep this conversation entirely to myself, whatever the outcome. Will you tell me what it is you want of me?"

Jane subsided into a chair, tears of excitement springing into her eyes.

"Well, you see, it's pretty serious business," she said, making a dab at the corner of one eye. "I thought I could trust you, or I wouldn't a come. But you gotta take me on trust, too."

"Of course," said Reyburn. "Now, what have you to do with this girl? Do you know where she is?"

"I certainly do!" said Jane, "but I ain't a-goin' ta tell until you say if there's anything you can do fer her. 'Cause you see, if you can't find a way to help her, I've gotta do it myself, an' it might get you into trouble somehow fer you to know what you ain't supposed to know."

"I see," said Reyburn, meekly. "Well, what are you going to tell me? Am I allowed to ask that?"

Jane grinned.

"Say, you're kiddin' me! I guess you are all right. Well, I'll just tell you about it. One night last November—you can see the date there in the paper, I was goin' home to my boardin' house in Camac Street, an' I was passin' the side of that church on Eighteenth an' Spruce, where the weddin' was—you know, fer you was there!"

Reyburn looked at her astonished.

"How did you know I was there?"

"I saw you through the window, over against the wall to the street side of the altar," said Jane calmly.

"How did you know me?"

"Oh, somebody I know pointed you out once an' said you was goin' to be one of the risin' lawyers of the day," she answered nonchalantly, her face quite serious.

A flicker of amusement passed like a ray of light through his eyes, but his face was entirely grave as he ignored the compliment.

"Go on!"

"I saw there was a weddin' an' I stopped to watch a minute, 'cause I expect to get married myself some day, an' I wanted to see how they did things. But I couldn't get near the door, an' the windows were all high up. I could only see folks who were standing up like you were. So I thought I'd go on. I turned the corner and went longside the church listenin' to the music, an' just as I passed a big iron gate at the back of the church somebody grabbed me an' begged me to help 'em. I looked round, an' there was the bride, all in her white togs, with the prettiest white satin slippers, in the wet an' mud! I tried to get her line, but she cried out somebody was comin' back in the passageway, so I slipped off my coat an' hat and whisked her into 'em an' clapped my rubbers over her satin shoes, and we beat it round the corner. I took her to my room, an' gave her some supper. She was all in. Then I put her to bed, an' she told me a little bit about it. She didn't tell me much. Only that they had been tryin' fer a long time back to make her marry a man she hated, an' now they'd almost tricked her into it, an' she'd die if she had to do it. She wanted to exchange clothes with me, 'cause, of course, she couldn't get anywhere togged out that way, so we changed things, an' fixed her up. In the mornin' I ran out an' got a paper, an' found they was sayin' she was temporary insane, an' stuff like that, an' so I saw their game was tryin' to get her in a 'sylum till they could make her do what they wanted. I fixed her up an' got her off to a place I know where she'd be safe. An' she's got a job an' doin' real well. But now they've got this here reward business out everywhere in the papers an' the movies, she ain't safe nowhere. An' I want somebody that's wiser'n me to take a holt an' do somethin'. I can't pay much, but I'll pay a little every month as long's I live ef it takes that long to pay yer bill, an' I have a notion she may have some money herself, though she didn't say nothin' about it. But there's a ring she left with me to sell, to pay fer what I gave her. It oughtta be worth somethin'. It looks real. I ain't sold it. I couldn't. I thought she might want it sometime—"

But Reyburn interrupted her excitedly.

"Do you mean to say that Miss Stanhope is in the city and you know where she is?"

"Now, don't get excited," warned Jane coolly. "I didn't say she was in this city, did I? I didn't say where she was, did I? I said she was safe."

"But are you aware that you have told me a very strange story? What proof can you give me that it is true?"

Jane looked at him indignantly.

"Say, I thought you was goin' to trust me? I have to trust you, don't I? Course you don't know who I am, an' I haven't told you, but I've got a good p'sition myself, an' I don't go round tellin' privarications! An' there's the weddin' dress, an' veil and fixin's! I got them. You can see 'em if you like— that is pervided I know what you're up to! I ain't taking any chances till I see what you mean to do."

"I beg your pardon," said Reyburn, trying to smile assurance once more. "You certainly must own this whole thing is enough to make anybody doubt."

"Yes, it is," said Jane. "I was some upset myself, havin' a thing like that happen to me, a real millionairess bride drop herself down on my hands just like that, an' I s'pose it *is* hard to b'lieve. But I can't waste much more time now. I gotta get back to my job. Is there anything can be done to keep 'em from gettin' her again?"

"I should most certainly think so," said Reyburn, "but I would have to know her side of the story, the whole of it, before I could say just what!"

"Well, s'pose you found there wasn't anythin' you could do to help her, would you go an' tell on her?"

Reyburn leaned back in his chair and smiled at his unique client:

"I shall have to quote your own language. 'What do you take me for?'"

"A white man!" said Jane suddenly, and showed all her fine teeth in an engaging smile. "Say, you're all right. Now, I gotta go. When will you tell me what you can do?" She glanced anxiously at her little leather-bound wrist watch. It was almost time for Jimmie to return. Jimmie mustn't find her here. He wouldn't understand, and what Jimmie didn't know wouldn't hurt him.

"Well, this ought to be attended to, at once, if anything is to be done," he said eagerly. "Let me see. I have an engagement at five. How would seven o'clock do? Could I call at your boardinghouse? Would there be any place where we could talk uninterrupted?"

"Sure," said Jane, rising. "I'll get my landlady to let me have her settin' room fer an hour."

"Meantime, I'll think it over and try to plan something."

Jane started down the long flights of stairs, not daring to trust to the elevator, lest she should come face to face with Jimmie and have to explain.

Reyburn stood with his back to the room, his hands in his pockets, frowning and looking out the window, when Jimmie entered a moment later.

"I hope I'm not late, sir?" he said anxiously, as he hung up his hat and sat down at his typewriter. "I had to wait. The man was out."

"Oh, that's all right, Ryan," said his employer, obviously not listening to his explanation. "I'm going out now, Ryan. I may not be back this afternoon. Just see that everything is all right."

"Very well, sir."

Reyburn went out, then opened the door and put his head back in the room.

"I may have to go out of town tonight, Ryan. I'm not sure. Something has come up. If I'm not in tomorrow, could you—would you mind just staying here all day and looking after things? I may need you. Of course you'll lock up and leave the card out when you go to lunch."

"Very well, sir."

"I'll keep in touch with you in case I'm delayed," and Reyburn was off again. When the elevator had clanked down to the next floor Jimmie went to the window and looked dreamily out over the roofs of the city:

"Aw!" he breathed joyously. "Now I'll bet he's going to do something about that reward!"

Reyburn hurried down the street to the office of an old friend where he had a bit of business as an excuse, and asked a few casual questions when he was done. Then he went on to a telephone booth and called up a friend of his mother's, with whom he had a brief gossip, ostensibly to give a message from his mother, contained in her last letter to him. None of the questions that he asked were notice-able. He merely led the conversation into certain grooves. The lady was an old resident and well known in the higher social circles. She knew all there was to know about every-body and she loved to tell it. She never dreamed that he had any motive in leading her on.

He dropped into a bank and asked a few questions, called up an address they gave him and made another inquiry, then dropped around to his cousin's home for a few min-utes, where he allowed her to tell all she knew about the Stanhope wedding they had attended together, and the dif-ferent theories concerning the escaped bride. Quite casu-ally he asked if she knew whether the bride had property of her own, if so who were her guardians. His cousin thought she knew a lot, but, sifting it down, he discovered that it was nearly all hearsay or surmise.

When he reached Jane Carson's boardinghouse he found that young woman ensconced in a tiny room, nine by twelve, a faded ingrain carpet on the floor, a depressed looking bed lounge against the bleary wallpaper, beneath crayon portraits of the landlady's dead husband and sons. There was a rocking chair, a trunk, a cane-seat chair, and an oil stove turned up to smoking point in honor of the caller, but there was little room left for the caller. On the top of the trunk reposed a large pasteboard box securely tied.

Jane, after a shy greeting, untied the strings and opened the cover, having first carefully slipped the bolt of the door.

"You can't be too careful," she said. "You never can tell."

Reyburn stood beside her and looked in a kind of awe at the glistening white, recognized the thick texture of the satin, the rare quality of the rosepoint lace with which it was adorned, caught the faint fragrance of faded orange blossoms wafting from the filmy mist of the veil as Jane lifted it tenderly; then leaned over and touched a finger to the pile of whiteness, reverently as though he were paying a tribute at a lovely shrine.

Jane even unwrapped the little slippers, one at a time, and folded them away again, and they said no word until it was all tied back in its papers, Reyburn assisting with the strings.

"Now, ef you don't mind waitin' a minute I guess it would be safer to put it away now," she said as she slipped the bolt and ran upstairs.

She was back in a minute and sat down opposite to him, drawing out from the neck of her blouse a ribbon with a heavy glittering circlet at its end.

"Here's the ring." She laid it in his palm. He took it, wondering, a kind of awe still upon him that he should be thus handling the intimate belongings of that little unknown bride whom he had seen lying unconscious in a strange church a few short months before. How strange that all this should have come to him when many wiser, more nearly related, were trying their best to get some clue to the mystery!

He lifted the ring toward the insufficient gas jet to make out the initials inside, and copied them down in his notebook.

"Take good care of that. It is valuable," he said as he handed it back to her.

"Mebbe I better give it to you," she half hesitated.

"You've taken pretty good care of it so far," he said. "I guess you've a better right to it than I. Only don't let anybody know you've got it. Now, I've been making inquiries, and I've found out a few things, but I've about come to the conclusion that I can't do much without seeing the lady. Do you suppose she would see me? Is she very far away?"

"When do you want to go?" asked Jane.

"At once," he answered decidedly. "There's no time to waste if she is really in danger, as you think."

Jane's eyes glittered with satisfaction.

"There's a train at ten-thirty. You'll get there in the morning. I've written it all down here on a paper so you can't make any mistakes. I've written her a letter so she'll understand and tell you everythin'. I'll wire Ma, too, so she'll let you see her. Ma might not size you up right."

Reyburn wondered at the way he accepted his orders from this coolly impudent girl, but he liked her in spite of himself.

In a few minutes more he was out in the street again, hurrying to his own apartment, where he put together a few necessities in a bag and went to the train.

Chapter 12

It was one of those little ironies of fate that are spoken about so much, that when Warren Reyburn alighted from the train in Tinsdale, Abijah Gage should be supporting one corner of the station, and contributing a quid now and then to the accumulations of the week scattered all about his feet.

He spotted the stranger at once and turned his cunning little eyes upon him, making it obvious that he was bulging with information. It was, therefore, quite natural, when Reyburn paused to take his bearings, that Bi should speak up and inquire if he was looking for someone. Reyburn shook his head and passed on, but Bi was not to be headed off so easily as that. He shuffled after him:

"Say!" he said, pointing to a shackley horse and buckboard that stood near, belonging to a pal over at the freight house. "Ef you want a lift I'll take you along."

"Thank you, no," said Reyburn, smiling; "I'm not going far."

"Say!" said Bi again as he saw his quarry about to disappear. "You name ain't Bains, is it?"

"No!" said Reyburn, quite annoyed by the persistent old fellow.

"From New York?" he hazarded cheerfully.

"No," answered Reyburn, turning to go. "You must excuse me. I'm in a hurry."

"That's all right," said Bi contentedly. "I'll walk a piece with you. I was lookin' fer a doctor to take down to see a sick

94

child. A doctor from New York. You ain't by any chance a doctor, are you?" Bi eyed the big leather bag inquiringly.

"No," said Reyburn, laughing in spite of his annoyance. "I'm only a lawyer." And with a bound he cleared the curb and hurried off down the street, having now recognized the direction described in Jane's diagram of Tinsdale.

Abijah Gage looked after him with twinkling eyes of dry mirth, and slowly sauntered after him, watching him until he entered the little unpainted gate of the Carson house and tapped at the old gray door. Then Bi lunged across the street and entered a path that ran along the railroad track for a few rods, curving suddenly into a stretch of vacant lots. On a convenient fence rail with a good outlook toward the west end of the village he ensconced himself and set about whittling a whistle from some willow stalks. He waited until he saw Bobbie Carson hurry off toward Hathaway's house and return with Lizzie Hope; waited hopefully until the stranger finally came out of the house again, touched his hat gracefully to the girl as she stood at the open door. Then he hurried back to the station again, and was comfortably settled on a tub of butter just arrived by freight, when Reyburn reached there. He was much occupied with his whistle, and never seemed to notice, but not a movement of the stranger escaped him, and when the Philadelphia express came by, and the stranger got aboard the parlor car, old Bi Gage swung his lumbering length up on the back platform of the last car. The hounds were hot on the trail now.

It was several years since Bi Gage had been on so long a journey, but he managed to enjoy the trip, and kept in pretty good touch with the parlor car, although he was never in evidence. If anybody had told Warren Reyburn as he let himself into his apartment late that night that he was being followed, he would have laughed and told them it was an impossibility. When he came out to the street the next morning and swung himself into a car that would land him at his office, he did not see the lank flabby figure of the toothless Bi standing just across the block, and keeping tab on him from the back platform, nor notice that he slid into the office building behind him and took the same elevator up, crowding in behind two fat men and effacing himself against the wall of the cage. Reyburn was reading his paper, and did not look up. The figure slid out of the elevator after him and slithered into a shadow, watching him, slipping softly after, until sure which door he took, then waited silently until sure that the door was shut. No one heard the slouching footsteps come down the marble hall. Bi Gage always wore rubbers when he went anywhere in particular. He had them on that morning. He took careful note of the name on the door: "*Warren Reyburn*, Attorney-at-Law," and the number. Then he slid down the stairs as unobserved as he had come, and made his way to a name and number on a bit of paper from his pocket which he consulted in the shelter of a doorway.

When Warren Reyburn started on his first trip to Tinsdale his mind was filled with varying emotions. He had never been able to quite get away from the impression made upon him by that little white bride lying so still amid her bridal finery, and the glowering bridegroom above her. It epitomized for him all the unhappy marriages of the world, and he felt like starting out somehow in hot pursuit of that bridegroom and making him answer for the sadness of his bride. Whenever the matter had been brought to his memory he had always been conscious of the first gladness he had felt when he knew she had escaped. It could not seem to him anything but a happy escape, little as he knew about any of the people who played the principal parts in the little tragedy he had witnessed.

Hour after hour as he sat in the train and tried to sleep or tried to think he kept wondering at himself that he was going on this wild goose chase, as he called it in his innermost thoughts. Yet he knew he had to go. In fact, he had known it from the moment James Ryan had shown him the advertisement. Not that he had ever had any idea of trying for that horrible reward. Simply that his soul had been stirred to its most knightly depths to try somehow to protect her in her hiding. Of course, it had been a mere crazy thought then, with no way of fulfillment, but when the

chance had offered of really finding her and asking if there
was anything she would like done, he knew from the instant
it was suggested that he was going to do it, even if he lost
every other business chance he ever had or expected to
have, even if it took all his time and every cent he could
borrow. He knew he had to try to find that girl! The thought
that the only shelter between her and the great awful world
lay in the word of an untaught girl like Jane Carson filled
him with terror for her. If that was true, the sooner someone
of responsibility and sense got to her the better. The questions he had asked of various people that afternoon had revealed more than he had already guessed of the character of
the bridegroom to whom he had taken such a strong dislike
on first sight.

Thus he argued the long night through between the fitful
naps he caught when he was not wondering if he should find
her, and whether he would know her from that one brief
sight of her in church. How did he know but this was some
game put up on him to get him into a mix-up? He must go
cautiously, and on no account do anything rash or make any
promises until he had first found out all about her.

When morning dawned he was in a state of perturbation
quite unusual for the son and grandson of renowned lawyers
noted for their calmness and poise under all circumstances.
This perhaps was why the little incident with Abijah Gage
at the station annoyed him so extremely. He felt he was
doing a questionable thing in taking this journey at all. He
certainly did not intend to reveal his identity or business to
this curious old man.

The little gray house looked exactly as Jane had described
it, and as he opened the gate and heard the rusty chain that
held it clank he had a sense of having been there before.

He was pleasantly surprised, however when the door was
opened by Emily, who smiled at him out of shy blue eyes,
and stood waiting to see what he wanted. It was like expecting a viper and finding a flower. Somehow he had not antici-
pated anything flowerlike in Jane's family. The mother, too,
was a surprise when she came from her ironing, and, push-
ing her wavy gray hair back from a furrowed brow, lifted

intelligent eyes that reminded him of Jane, to search his face. Ma did not appear flustered. She seemed to be taking account of him and deciding whether or not she would be cordial to him.

"Yes, I had a telegram from Jane this moring." She was scanning his eyes once more to see whether there was a shadow of what she called shiftiness in them. "Come in," she added grudgingly.

He was not led into the dining room, but seated on one of the best varnished chairs in the parlor, as they called the little unused front room. He felt strangely ill at ease and began to be convinced that he was on the very wildest of goose chases. To think of expecting to find Elizabeth Stanhope in a place like this! If she ever had been here she certainly must have flown faster than she had from the church on her wedding night.

So, instead of beginning as he had planned, to put a list of logically prepared keen questions to a floundering and suspecting victim, he found the clear eyes of Ma looking into his unwaveringly and the wise tongue of Ma putting him through a regular orgy of catechism before she would so much as admit that she had ever heard of a girl named Lizzie Hope. Then he bethought him of her daughter's letter and handed it over for her to read.

"Well," she admitted at last, half satisfied, "she isn't here at present. I sent her away when I found you was comin'. I wasn't sure I'd let you see her at all if I didn't like your looks."

"That's right, Mrs. Carson," he said heartily, with real admiration in his voice. "I'm glad she has someone so careful to look out for her. Your daughter said she was in a good safe place, and I begin to see she knew what she was talking about."

Then the strong look around Ma's lips settled into the sweeter one, and she sent Bob after the girl.

"Are you a friend of hers?" she asked, watching him keenly.

"No," said Reyburn. "I've seen her but once. She doesn't know me at all."

"Are you a friend of her—family?"

"Oh, no!"

"Or any of her friends or relations?" Ma meant to be comprehensive.

"No. I'm sorry I am not. I am a rather recent comer to the city where she made her home, I understand."

Ma looked at him thoughtfully for a moment. It wouldn't have been called a stare, it was too kindly for that, but Reyburn thought to himself that he would not have liked to have borne her scrutiny if he had anything to conceal, for he felt as if she might read the truth in his eyes.

"Are you—please excuse me for askin'—but are you a member of any church?"

Reyburn flushed, and wanted to laugh, but was embarrassed in spite of himself:

"Why, yes—I'm a member," he said slowly, then with a frank lifting of his eyes to her troubled gaze, "I united with the church when I was a mere kid, but I'm afraid I'm not much of a member. I really am not what you'd call 'working' at it much nowadays. I go to morning service sometimes, but that's about all. I don't want to be a hypocrite."

He wondered as he spoke why he took the trouble to answer the woman so fully. Her question was in a way impertinent, much like the way her daughter talked. Yet she seemed wholly unconscious of it.

"I know," she assented sorrowfully. "There's lots of them in the church. We have 'em, too, even in our little village. But still, after all, you can't help havin' confidence more in them that has 'named the name' than in them that has not."

Reyburn looked at her curiously and felt a sudden infusion of respect for her. She was putting the test of her faith to him, and he knew by the little stifled sigh that he had been found wanting.

"I s'pose lawyers don't have much time to think about being Christians," she apologized for him.

He felt impelled to be frank with her:

"I'm afraid I can't urge that excuse. Unfortunately I have a good deal of time on my hands now. I've just opened my office and I'm waiting for clients."

"Where were you before that? You did not just get through studying?"

He saw she was wondering whether he was wise enough to help her protégée.

"No, I spent the last three years in France."

"Up at the front?" The pupils of her eyes dilated eagerly.

"Yes, in every drive," he answered, wondering that a woman of this sort should be so interested now that the war was over.

"And you came back safe!" she said slowly, looking at him with a kind of wistful sorrow in her eyes. "My boy was shot the first day he went over the top."

"Oh, I'm sorry," said Reyburn gently, a sudden tightness in his throat.

"But it was all right." She flashed a dazzling smile at him through the tears that came into her eyes. "It wasn't as if he wasn't ready. Johnny was always a good boy, an' he joined church when he was fourteen, an' always kep' his promises. He used to pray every night just as faithful, an' read his Bible. I've got the little Testament he carried all through. His chaplain sent it to me. It's got a bullet hole through it, and blood marks, but it's good to me to look at, 'cause I know Johnny's with his Saviour. He wasn't afraid to die. He said to me before he left, he says: 'Ma, if anythin' happens to me it's all right. You know, Ma, I ain't forgettin' what you taught me an' I ain't forgettin' Christ is with me.'"

Mrs. Carson wiped her eyes furtively, and tried to look cheerful. Reyburn wished he knew how to comfort her.

"It makes a man feel mean," he said at last, trying to fit his toe into the pattern of the ingrain carpet, "to come home alive and whole when so many poor fellows had to give their lives. I've often wondered how I happened to get through."

She looked at him tenderly:

"Perhaps your heavenly Father brought you back to give you more chance to do things for Him, an' get ready to die when your time comes."

There was something startling to this self-composed city chap in hearing a thing like this from the lips of the mother whose beloved son was gone forever beyond her teaching but had "been ready." Reyburn looked at her steadily, soberly, and then with a queer constriction in his throat he looked down at the floor thoughtfully and said:

"Perhaps He did."

"Well, I can't help bein' glad you're a church member, anyhow," said Mrs. Carson, rising to look out of the window. "She needs a Christian to help her, an' I'd sooner trust a Christian. If you really meant it when you joined church you've got somethin' to fall back on anyhow. Here she comes. I'll just go an' tell her you're in here."

Chapter 13

Betty, her eyes wide with fear, her face white as a lily, appeared like a wraith at the parlor door and looked at him. It gave Reyburn a queer sensation, as if a picture one had been looking at in a story book should suddenly become alive and move and stare at one. As he rose and came forward he still seemed to see like a dissolving view between them the little huddled bride on the floor of the church. Then he suddenly realized that she was trembling.

"Please don't be afraid of me, Miss Stanhope," he said gently. "I have only come to help you, and if after you have talked with me you feel that you would rather I should have nothing to do with your affairs I will go away and no one in the world shall be the wiser for it. I give you my word of honor."

"Oh!" said Betty, toppling into a chair near by. "I—guess—I'm not afraid of you. I just didn't know who you might be——!" She stopped, caught her breath and tried to laugh, but it ended sorrily, almost in a sob.

"Well, I don't wonder," said Reyburn, trying to find something reassuring to say. "The truth is, I was rather upset about you. I didn't quite know who you might turn out to be, you see!"

"Oh!" Betty's hand slipped up to her throat, and her lips quivered as she tried to smile.

"Please don't feel that way," he said, "or I'll go away at once." He was summoning all his courage and hoping she wasn't going to break down and cry. How little she was, and sweet! Her eyes pleaded, just as they did in that one look in the church. How could anybody be unkind to her?

"I'm quite all right," said Betty with a forced smile, sitting up very straight.

"Perhaps I'd better introduce myself," he said, trying to speak in a very commonplace tone. "I'm just a lawyer that your friend Miss Jane Carson sent out to see if I could be of any service to you. It may possibly make things a little easier for you if I explain that while I never had heard of you before, and have no possible connection with your family or friends, I happened to be at your wedding!"

"Oh!" said Betty with a little agonized breath.

"Do you know Mrs. Bryce Cochrane?" he asked.

Betty could not have got any whiter, but her eyes seemed to blanch a trifle.

"A little," she said in a very small voice.

"Well, she is my cousin."

"Oh!" said Betty again.

"Her husband was unable to accompany her to the wedding, and so I went in his place to escort Isabel. I knew nothing of your affairs either before or after the wedding, until this announcement was brought to my notice, and Miss Carson called on me."

Betty took the paper in her trembling fingers, and looked into her own pictured eyes. Then everything seemed to swim before her for a moment. She pressed her hand against her throat and set her white lips firmly, looking up at the stranger with a sudden terror and comprehension.

"You want to get that five thousand dollars!" she said, speaking the words in a daze of trouble. "Oh, I haven't got five thousand dollars! Not now! But perhaps I could manage to get it if you would be good enough to wait just a little, till I can find a way. Oh, if you knew what it means to me!"

Warren Reyburn sprang to his feet in horror, a flame of anger leaping into his eyes.

"Five thousand dollars be hanged!" he said fiercely. "Do I look like that kind of fellow? It may seem awfully queer to you for an utter stranger to be butting into your affairs like this unless I did have some ulterior motive, but I swear to you that I have none. I came out here solely because I saw that you were in great likelihood of being found by the people from whom you had evidently run away. Miss Stanhope, I stood where I could watch your face when you came up the aisle at your wedding, and something in your eyes just before you dropped made me wish I could knock that bridegroom down and take care of you somehow until you got that hurt look out of your face. I know it was rather ridiculous for an utter stranger to presume so far, but when I saw that the sleuths were out after you, and when the knowledge of your whereabouts was put into my hands without the seeking, I wouldn't have been a man if I hadn't come and offered my services. I'm not a very great lawyer, nor even a very rising one, as your Miss Carson seems to think, but I'm a man with a soul to protect a woman who is in danger, and if that's you, I'm at your service. If not, you've only to say so and I'll take the next train home and keep my mouth shut!"

He took his watch out and looked at it hastily, although he had not the slightest idea what it registered, nor what time the next train for home left. He looked very tall and strong and commanding as he stood in his dignity waiting for her answer, and Betty looked up like a little child and trusted him.

"Oh! Please forgive me!" she cried. "I've been so frightened ever since Bob came after me. I couldn't think you had come for any good, because I didn't know anyone in the world who would want to help me."

"Certainly!" said Warren Reyburn with a lump in his throat, sitting down quickly to hide his emotion. "Please consider me a friend, and command me."

"Thank you," said Betty taking a deep breath and trying to crowd back the tears. "I'm afraid there isn't any way to help me, but I'm glad to have a friend, and I'm sorry I was so rude."

"You weren't rude, and that was a perfectly natural conclusion from my blundering beginning," he protested, looking at the adorable waves of hair that framed her soft cheeks. "But there is always a way to help people when they are in trouble, and I'm here to find out what it is. Do you think you could trust me enough to tell me what it's all about? Miss Carson didn't seem to know much or else she didn't feel free to say."

"I didn't tell her much," said Betty, lifting her sea-blue eyes. "She was a stranger, too, you know."

"Well, she's a mighty good friend of yours, I'll say, and she's acted in a very wise manner. She took more precautions than an old detective would have done. She told me only that someone was trying to make you marry a man you did not wish to marry. Is that correct?"

Betty shivered involuntarily and a wave of color went over her white face.

"It sounds queer," she said, "as if I hadn't any character or force myself, but you don't understand. No one would understand unless they knew it all, and and been through it for years. At first I didn't quite understand it myself. I'd better tell you the story. I thought I never could tell anyone, because they were my father's family, and I know he would shrink so from having it known, but I'm sure he wouldn't blame me now."

"He certainly would not blame you, Miss Stanhope. I have heard that your father was a wonderful man, with high principles. I feel sure he would justify you in appealing to someone who was willing to advise you in a strait like this. You know no woman need ever marry any man against her will."

"Not if it were her father's dying wish?"

"Certainly not. Miss Stanhope, did your father love you?"

"Oh, I'm sure he did. He was the most wonderful father! I've often thought that he would never have asked it of me if he had realized——"

"Did he ever during his lifetime seem to wish you to be unhappy?"

"Never! That was the strange part of it. But you see he didn't know how I felt. I think I'd better tell you all about it."

"That would be the better way, if it won't be too hard for you."

Betty clasped her small hands together tightly and began:

"My own mother died when I was quite a little girl, so Father and I were a great deal to each other. He used to look after my lessons himself, and was always very careful what kind of teachers I had. He was mother and father both to me. When I was ten years old my governess died suddenly while Father was away on a business trip, and one of our neighbors was very kind to me, coming in and looking after the servants and everything and keeping me over at her house for a few days till Father got back. She had a widowed sister visiting her, a rather young woman who was very beautiful. At least I thought she was beautiful then, and she made a great pet of me, so that I grew fond of her, although I had not liked her at first.

"After Father came home she used to slip over every day to see me while he was at his business, and he was grateful to her for making me happy. Then he found out that she was in trouble, had lost her money or something, and wanted to get a position teaching. He arranged to have her teach me, and so she came to our house to stay.

"Somehow after that I never seemed to see so much of my father as I used to do, for she was always there, but at first I didn't care, because she was nice to me, and always getting up things to keep me busy and happy. She would make my father buy expensive toys and books and games for me, and fine clothes, and so of course I was pleased. In about a year my father married her, and at first it seemed very beautiful to me to have a real mother, but little by little I began to see that she preferred to be alone with my father and did not want me around so much. It was very hard to give up the companionship of my father, but my stepmother kept me busy with other things, so that I really didn't think much about it while it was first happening.

"But one day there came a letter. I remember it came while we were at breakfast, and my father got very white and stern when he read it, and handed it over to my stepmother and asked whether it was true, and then she began to cry and sent me from the table. I found out a few days after that that my stepmother had two sons, both older than myself, and that she had not told my father. It was through some trouble they had got into at school which required quite a large sum of money to cover damages that my father discovered it, and he was terribly hurt that she should have concealed it from him. I learned all this from the servants, who talked when they thought I was not within hearing. There were days and days when my father scarcely spoke at the table, and when he looked at me it made a pain go through my heart, he looked so stern and sad. My stepmother stayed a great deal in her room and looked as if she had been crying. But after a few weeks things settled down a good deal as they had been, only that my father never lost that sad troubled look. There was some trouble about my stepmother's sons, too, for there was a great deal of argument between her and my father, of which I only heard snatches, and then one day they came home to stay with us. Something had happened at the school where they were that they could not stay any longer. I can remember distinctly the first night they ate dinner with us. It seemed to me that it was like a terrific thunderstorm that never quite broke. Everybody was trying to be nice and polite, but underneath it all there was a kind of lightning of all kinds of feelings, hurt feelings and wrong ones and right ones all mixed up.

"Only the two boys didn't seem to feel it much. They sort of took things for granted, as if that had always been their home, and they didn't act very polite. It seemed to trouble my father, who looked at them so severely that it almost choked me, and I couldn't go on eating my dinner. He didn't seem like my dear father when he looked like that. I always used to watch my father, and he seemed to make the day for me. If he was sad, then I was sad; and if he was glad then I was happy all over, until one day my stepmother noticed me and said: 'See, dear little Elizabeth is trembling. You ought not to speak that way before her, Charles.' And then father looked at me, and all suddenly I learned to smile when I didn't feel like it. I smiled back to him just to let him know it didn't matter what he did, I would love him anyhow!"

During the recital Reyburn had sat with courteous averted gaze as though he would not trouble her with more of his presence than was absolutely necessary, now he gave her a swift glance.

Betty's eyes were off on distance, and she was talking from the depths of her heart, great tears welling into her eyes. All at once she remembered the stranger:

"I beg your pardon," she said, and brushed her hand across her eyes. "I haven't gone over it to anyone ever, and I forgot you would not be interested in details."

"Please don't mind me. I am interested in every detail you are good enough to give me. It all makes the background of the truth, you know, and that is what I am after," said Reyburn, deeply touched. "I think you are wonderful to tell me all this. I shall regard it most sacredly."

Betty flashed a look of gratitude at him, and noticed the sympathy in his face. It almost unnerved her, but she went on:

"The oldest boy was named Bessemer, and he wasn't very good-looking. He was very tall and awkward, always falling over things. He had little pale eyes, and hardly any chin. His teeth projected, too, and his hair was light and very straight and thin. His mother didn't seem to love him very much, even when he was a little boy. She bullied him and found fault with him continually, and quite often I felt very sorry for him, although I wasn't naturally attracted to him. He wasn't really unpleasant to me. We got along very nicely, although I never had much to do with him. There wasn't much to him.

"The other brother, Herbert, was handsome like his mother, only dark, with black curly hair, black wicked eyes, and a big, loose, cruel mouth. His mother just idolized him, and he knew it. He could make her do anything on earth. He used to force Bessemer into doing wrong things, too, things that he was afraid to do himself, because he knew Father would not be so hard on Bessemer as on him. For

Father had taken a great dislike to Herbert, and it was no wonder. He seemed to have no idea at all that he was not owner of the house. He took anything he pleased for his own use, even Father's most sacred possessions, and broke them in a fit of anger, too, sometimes, without ever saying he was sorry. He talked very disrespectfully of Father and to him, and acted so to the servants that they gave notice and left. Every few days there would be a terrible time over something Herbert had done. Once I remember he went to the safe and got some money out that belonged to Father and went off and spent it in some dreadful way that made Father very angry. Of course I was still only a little girl, and I did not know all that went on. Father was very careful that I should not know. He guarded me more than ever, but he always looked sad when he came to kiss me good-night.

"Herbert took especial delight in tormenting me," she went on with a sad faraway look in her eyes as if she were recalling unpleasant memories. She did not see the set look on Reyburn's face nor notice his low exclamation of anger. She went steadily on: "He found out that I did not like june bugs, and once he caught hundreds of them and locked me into a room with them with all the lights turned on. I was almost frightened to death, but it cured me of being afraid of june bugs." A little smile trembled out on Betty's lips. "Just because I wouldn't give him the satisfaction of letting him hear me scream," she finished. "Then he caught a snake and put it in my room, and he put a lot of burdocks in my hat so they would get in my hair. Foolish things those were, of course, but he was a constant nightmare to me. Sometimes he would tie a wire across the passages in the upper hall where I had to pass to my room, and when I fell my hands went down against a lot of slimy toads in the dark, for he always somehow managed to have the light go out just as I fell. There were hundreds of things like that, but I needn't multiply them. That's the kind of boy he was. And because he discovered that my father loved me very much, and because he knew my father disliked him, he spent much time in trying to torment me in secret. I couldn't tell my father, because he always looked so sad whenever there was trouble, and there was sure to be trouble between him and my stepmother if my father found out that Herbert had done anything wrong. One day my father came upon us just as Herbert had caught me and was trying to cut my curls off. I didn't care about the curls, but I knew my father did. I began to scream. Herbert gripped me so I thought I would die with the pain, putting his big strong fingers around my throat and choking me so I could not make any noise."

Reyburn clenched his hands until the knuckles went white and uttered an exclamation, but Betty did not notice:

"There was a terrible time then, and I was sent away to a school, a good many miles from home, where I stayed for several years. Father always came up to see me every week-end, for a few hours at least, and we had wonderful times together. Sometimes on vacation he would bring my step-mother along and she would bring me beautiful presents and smile and pet me, and say she missed me so much and she wished I would ask my father to let me come back and go to school in the city. But I never did, because I was afraid of Herbert. As I grew older I used to have an awful horror of him. But finally one vacation Father and stepmother both came up and said they wanted me at home. My stepmother went to my room with me and told me I needn't be afraid of Herbert anymore, that he was quite grown-up and changed and would be good to me, and that it would please my father to have all his family together happily again. I believed her and I told Father I would like to go. He looked very happy, and so I went home. Herbert had been away at school himself most of the time, and so had Bessemer, although they had been in trouble a good many times, so the servants told me, and had to change to new schools. They were both away when I got home. I had a very happy time for three weeks, only that I never saw Father alone once. My stepmother was always there. But she was kind and I tried not to mind. Then all of a sudden one night I woke up and heard voices, and I knew that the boys were back from the camp to which they had been sent. I didn't sleep much the rest of the night, but in the morning I made up my mind that it was only a little while before I could go back to school, and I would be nice to the boys and maybe they wouldn't trouble me.

"I found that it was quite true that Herbert had grown up and changed. He didn't want to torment me anymore, he wanted to make love to me, and I was only a child yet. I wasn't quite fifteen. It filled me with horror, and after he had caught me in the dark—he always loved to get people in the dark—and tried to kiss me, I asked Father to let me go back to school at once. I can remember how sad he looked at me as if I had cut him in the heart when I asked him."

During this part of the tale Reyburn sat with stern countenance, his fingers clenched around the arms of the chair in which he sat, but he held himself quiet and listened with compressed lips, watching every expression that flitted across the sweet pale face.

"That was the last time I was at home with my father," she said, trying to control her quivering lips. "He took me back to school, and he came three times to see me, though not so often as before. The last time he said beautiful things to me about trying to live a right life and being kind to those about me, and he asked me to forgive him if he had ever done anything to hurt me in any way. Of course I said he hadn't. And then he said he hoped I wouldn't feel too hard at him for marrying again and bringing those boys into my life. I told him it was all right, that someday they would grow up and go away and he and I would live together again! And he said some awful words about them under his breath. But he asked me to forgive him again and kissed me and went away.

"He was taken very sick when he got home, and they never let me know until he was dead. Of course I went home to the funeral, but I didn't stay; I couldn't. I went back to school alone. My stepmother had been very kind, but she said she knew it was my father's wish that I should finish my school year. When vacation came she was traveling for her health. She wrote me a beautiful letter telling me how she missed me, and how much she needed me now in her bereavement, and how she hoped another summer would see us together; but she stayed abroad two years and the third year she went to California. I was sent to another school, and because I was not asked about it and there didn't seem anything else to do, I went. Every time I would suggest doing something else my stepmother would write and say how sorry she was she could not give her consent, but my father had left very explicit directions about me and she was only trying to carry out his wishes. She knew me well enough to be sure I would want to do anything he wished for me. And I did, of course."

Reyburn gave her a look of sympathy and getting up began to pace the little room.

Chapter 14

"It was not until last spring that she sent for me to come home," went on Betty, "and was very effusive about how much she needed me and how she was so much better, and meant to be a real mother to me now, helping me see the world and have a good time. She took me from one summer resort to another. Of course it was pleasant after having been shut up in school all those years, but she kept me close with her all the time, and I met only the people she chose to have me meet. All the time she kept talking about 'dear Herbert' and telling how wonderful he was and how he had grown to be 'such a dear boy.' Finally he arrived and began the very first evening he was with us to coax me to marry him. At first he was very courteous and waited upon me whenever I stirred, and I almost thought his mother was right about his being changed. But when I told him that I did not love him and could not ever marry him I caught a look on his face like an angry snarl, and I heard him tell his mother I was a crazy little fool, and that he would break my neck for me after he got me good and married. Then his mother began to come to me and cry and tell me how dear Herbert was almost heartbroken, that he would never lift up his head again, and that I would send him to ruin. It was simply awful, and I didn't know how to endure it. I began to wonder where I could go. Of course I had never been brought up to do anything, so I could not very well expect to go out into the world and make my living."

"Didn't you have any money at all?" interrupted Reyburn suddenly.

"Oh, yes," she said, looking up as if she had just remembered his presence. "I had always plenty of spending money, but if I went away where they couldn't find me, why, of course, I would have to give that up."

"Why, where did your money come from? Was it an allowance from your stepmother, or did your father leave it to you, or what?"

"I'm not just sure," said Betty, with troubled brow. "I never really knew much about the money affairs. When I asked, they always put me off and said that I was too young to be bothered with business yet, I would be told all about it when I came of age. My stepmother harped a great deal on keeping me young as long as possible. She said it was my father's wish that I should be relieved of all care until I came of age. But there were some trustees in Boston. I know that, because I had to write to them, about once or twice a year. My stepmother was most particular about that. I think they were old friends of my own mother, though I don't know when I learned that. Father told me once that Mother had left me enough to keep me comfortably even without what he would leave me, so I'm sure I shall have enough to repay you if I could once get it."

"Don't worry about me!" he exclaimed. "It seems so terrible for you to have been alone in a situation like that! Wasn't there anyone you could appeal to for help?"

"No, not anyone whom I thought it would be right to tell. You see, in a way it was my father's honor. She was his wife, and I'm sure he loved her—at least at first—and she really was very good to me, except when it was a question of her son."

"I'm afraid I can't agree with you there!" he said sternly. "I think she was a clever actress. But excuse me. Go on, please."

"At last, when things had got so bad that I thought I must run away somewhere, my stepmother came into my room one morning and locked the door. She had been weeping, and she looked very sweet and pitiful. She said she had something to tell me. She had tried not to have to do it, for she was afraid it would grieve me and might make me have hard feelings against my father. I told her that was impossible. Then she told me that my father on his deathbed had called her to him and told her that it was his wish that I should marry one of her sons, and he wanted her to tell me. He felt that he had wronged them by hating them for my sake and he felt that I could make it all right by marrying one of them. My stepmother said that when she saw how infatuated dear Herbert was with me she hoped that she would be spared having to tell me, but now that I was treating him so she felt bound to deliver the message. Then she handed me a paper which said virtually the same thing which she had told me, and was signed by my father in his own handwriting."

"Was the paper written or printed?" interrupted Reyburn.

"I think it was typewritten, but the signature was Papa's. There could be no mistake about that, and he wouldn't have signed something he didn't mean." Betty sighed as if it were a subject she had worn into her heart by much sorrowful thought.

"It might be quite possible for him to have done that under influence or delirium, or when he was too sick to realize."

"Oh, do you think so?" Betty caught at the hope. "It seems so awful to go against Papa's last request."

"There is nothing awful but the idea of your being tied to that—beast!" said Reyburn with unexpected fervor. Betty looked at him gratefully and went on:

"I was simply appalled. I couldn't think, and I made my stepmother go away and leave me for a little while, but things got blacker and blacker and I thought I was going crazy. I couldn't marry Herbert even to please my father. The next day Bessemer arrived. He had been worrying his mother a lot about money, and when he arrived I couldn't help hearing what they said to him. They charged him with all sort of dreadful things. They called him a disgrace, and threatened to let him be arrested, and a great many more such things. Finally his mother ended up by telling him she never had loved him and that if he made any more trouble about money she would cut him off without a cent. I was sitting upstairs in my room with my windows open, and all their talk floated right up to me. It made me feel sick, and yet I felt sorry for Bessemer, for lately whenever he had been around he had been kind to me, and sometimes I had stayed near him to get rid of Herbert. We often talked over our troubles together and sympathized with one another. He felt sorry for me, but he was weak himself and couldn't see any way out for either of us.

"They had pretty stormy times all that day. Late in the afternoon Herbert and Bessemer went to their mother's room and were closeted with her for two hours, after which Herbert went away in the car with his suitcase and bags as if he were not coming back soon. I watched him from my window, and in great relief went down to take a little walk, for I had stayed closely in my room all day trying to plan what to do. One thing that held me from running away was that it would be such a disgrace to the family, and I knew my father would have felt it so keenly. That was always the great trouble when the boys got into scrapes at college, my father would groan and say he felt disgraced to be so conspicuous before the world. So I hesitated to do what would have been a sorrow to him had he been alive.

"Half an hour later I was sitting alone in the twilight on one of the porches, and Bessemer came out and sat down beside me.

"He looked so sort of homely and lonesome that I put my hand on his arm and told him I was awfully sorry for him, and suddenly he turned around and said:

"'Say, Betty, why don't you marry *me*? Then they can't say a word to either of us. Your father's wishes will be carried out and Herb'll have to whistle.'

"At first I was horrified, but we talked a long time about it, and he told me how lonely he had always been, and how nobody had ever loved him, and he knew he wasn't attractive, and all that; and then he said that if I married him we would go away and live by ourselves and he would let me do just as I wanted to. He wouldn't bother me about anything. If I didn't love him he would keep out of my sight, and things like that, till I got very sorry for him, and began to think that perhaps after all it was the best thing that would ever come for either of us. So I said I would.

"It surprised me a little that my stepmother took it so calmly when we told her. She cried a little, but did it very prettily, and kissed Bessemer, and told him he was fortunate. Then she kissed me and said I was a darling, and that she would be so happy if it only weren't for poor dear Herbert.

"But after that they began to rush things for a grand wedding, and I let them do it because I didn't see anything else in the world for me."

Betty raised her eyes and encountered the clear grave gaze of Reyburn fixed on her, and the color flew into her cheeks:

"I know you think I'm dreadful," she said, shrinking. "I've thought so myself a thousand times, but truly I didn't realize then what an awful thing it would be to marry a man I didn't love. I only wanted to hurry up and get it done before Herbert came home. They said he had been called away by important business and might be at home any day. I gave my consent to everything they wanted to do, and they fixed it all just as they pleased. One thing that happened upset me terribly. When the wedding invitations came home my stepmother carried them off to her room. I was too sad to pay much attention anyway. But the next morning I happened to be down in the kitchen looking over the papers that the maid had taken down from the waste baskets to search for a missing letter and there in the pile I found one of the invitations partly addressed and flung aside, and the invitation was still in the envelope. I pulled it out with a ghastly kind of curiosity to see how I looked on paper, and there it read, Mrs. Charles Garland Stanhope invites you to be present at the marriage of her daughter Elizabeth to *Mr. Herbert Hutton*!

"My heart just stood still. With the paper in my hand I rushed up to my stepmother's room and demanded to know what that meant. She smiled and said she was so sorry I had been annoyed that way, that that was a mistake, the invitations had come wrongly engraved and she had had to send them back and have them done over again. She was afraid I might be superstitious about it, so she hadn't told me. She was very gentle and sweet and tried to soothe me, and called me, 'Betty,' the name my father always had for me, and at last I went back to my room feeling quite comfortable. She had said she always felt troubled for poor Bessemer, that nobody could love him right, he was so homely, and now I was going to make everything right by marrying him. She was going to try to forget what I had done to poor dear Herbert, and just be happy about Bessemer. She talked so nicely that I kissed her, a thing I hadn't done in years, not since she was first married to Father. But somehow the shock of seeing Herbert's name on the invitation stayed with me, and I began to feel gloomier about it all and to wonder if perhaps I had done right. The last day I was terribly depressed and when I got to the church that night it suddenly came to me that perhaps after all I was not going to be free at all as I had hoped, but was just tying myself up to them all for life. I was thinking that as I walked up the aisle, and my throat had a big lump in it the way it always does when I'm frightened, and then I looked up hoping a glimpse of poor Bessemer's face would steady me and he wasn't there at all! And right over me, waiting beside the minister, to marry me stood *Herbert*! My knees just gave way under me, and everything got black so I couldn't go on another step, nor even stand up. I had to drop. I wasn't unconscious as you all thought—I heard everything that went on, but I couldn't do anything about it.

"After they had carried me into the other room and given me things to drink, and I could get my breath again I saw it all clearly. Herbert hadn't given up at all. He meant to marry me anyway. He had had the invitations printed with his name on purpose and they probably hadn't been changed at all. Everybody in that great church out there was *expecting* me to marry Herbert Hutton, and I *was not going to do it*! I didn't quite know how I was going to stop it, but I knew I had to! You see I was brought up to think a great deal about what people would think of me if I did anything out of the usual, and it seemed to me I had disgraced myself forever by dropping down in the aisle. I knew Herbert well enough to be sure he would carry that wedding through now if he had to hold me up in his arms till the ceremony was over, and I was desperate. I would have given everything I had in the world if the floor had opened and swallowed me up then, but of course I knew wild thoughts like that wouldn't get me anywhere, so I just shut my eyes and tried to think of a way; and then I asked them all to go out a minute and let me be quiet. The doctor who had come out of the church told them to go. I shall always bless that man, whoever he was! Then when they were gone I opened a door that had a key in it, and I locked it behind me and ran away down some stairs and out a passage that led to the street. That girl, Jane Carson, was passing and she put her own coat on me and took me to her room and sent me here. Oh, it's been so good to get here! Do you think they can take me away against my will?"

"Certainly not!" said the young man. "Not without some foul play, but I don't intend to give them any chance for that. By the way, when do you come of age?"

"In three weeks," said Betty, looking troubled. "Why, would I be safe after I was of age?"

"You certainly would not be under their guardianship any longer," said the lawyer, "and they would have no right to control your actions, unless of course you were incapacitated somehow and unfit to manage your own affairs."

Betty looked troubled.

"I've thought sometimes, ever since I saw that paper in which they hinted that I was temporarily insane, that they might try to shut me up in a mental hospital. Herbert wouldn't stop at anything. Could he do that?"

"They would have to get a doctor to swear that you were mentally unsound," said Reyburn, looking troubled. "Does he really love you, do you think or does he only want to get you in his power for some reason?"

"It is more like that," said Betty sorrowfully, "he couldn't really love anybody but himself."

"Well, don't you worry. I'm going at the case at once, and I'll put those people where they'll have to walk a chalk line before many hours are over. The first thing I must do is to see those trustees of yours. Can you give me the names and addresses?"

He got out his fountain pen, and Betty told him all he wanted to know, that is, all she knew herself, and then suddenly it was train time and he hurried away. On the steps he paused and said in a low tone:

"Are you perfectly comfortable with these people for a few days until I can get you better accommodations where you will be safe?"

"Entirely," said Betty eagerly. "I wouldn't want to go elsewhere."

"But it must be very hard for one like you to be thrown constantly with illiterate, uncultured people."

Betty smiled dreamily:

"I don't think they are exactly uncultured," she said slowly. "They—well, you see, they make a friend of God, and somehow I think that makes a difference. Don't you think it would?"

"I should think it would," said Warren Reyburn reverently with a light in his eyes. "I think, perhaps, if you don't mind my saying it, that you, too, have been making a friend of God."

"I've been trying to," said Betty softly, with a shy glow on her face that he remembered all the way back to the city.

Chapter 15

Candace Cameron paced her little gabled room restively, with face growing redder and more excited at every step. For several weeks now she had been virtually a prisoner—albeit a willing enough one—in the house of Stanhope. But the time had come when she felt that she must do something.

She had gone quietly enough about a proscribed part of the house, doing little helpful things, making herself most useful to the madam, slipping here and there with incredible catlike tread for so plump a body, managing to overhear important conversations, and melting away like a wraith before her presence was discovered. She had made herself so unobtrusive as to be almost forgotten by all save the maid Marie, who had been set to watch her; and she had learned that if she went to bed quite early in the evening, Marie relaxed her watch and went down to the servants' quarters, or even sometimes went out with a lover for awhile, that is, if the madam herself happened to be out also. On several such occasions she had made valuable tours of investigation through the madam's desk and private papers.

That she was overstepping her privileges as a servant in the house went without saying, but she silenced her Scotch conscience, which until this period of her existence had always kept her strictly from meddling with other people's affairs, by declaring over and over again to herself that she was doing perfectly right because she was doing it for the sake of "that poor wee thing that was being cheated of her rights."

Several weeks had passed since her sudden reestablishment in the family, and the reports of Betty, so hastily readjusted and refurbished to harmonize with the newspaper reports, had not been any more satisfying. Mrs. Stanhope had explained to the servants the day after the excitement that Miss Betty had become temporarily deranged, and later that she had escaped from the private hospital where she had been taken, and they were doing all in their power to find her. In reply to Candace's gimletlike questions she had given the name of a hospital where she said Betty had been taken at first, and everything seemed altogether plausible. But as the days went by and the horror of her absence grew into the soul of the lonely woman whose care Betty had been years, Candace became more and more restive and suspicious. It was these suspicions which sent her on her investigations, and made her uncannily wise to pry open secret locks and cover all trace of her absence after she had gleaned what knowledge she sought.

On this particular evening her excitement was due to having come across some correspondence bearing the signature of a man to whom a certain letter had been addressed, which had been entrusted to her charge by Betty's dying father and taken from her by his wife. For years she had been worried about that, and yet she had no absolute reason to doubt that the madam had not sent it to its destination, except as she knew its contents and read Mrs. Stanhope's character beneath the excellent camouflage. But tonight, even the briefest glance through the handle of letters showed plainly that those men in Boston never knew the master's wishes, or at least, if they knew them, they were utterly disregarding them.

Aroused on one point, her suspicions began to extend further. Where was Betty? Did her stepmother know, and was she somewhere suffering, alone, perhaps being neglected because she had not done as they wanted her to do? If the stepmother was capable of destroying a letter, was she perhaps not also capable of putting Betty out of the way?

There were points of detail which of course did not harmonize with any such theory as this. Candace was no logician, but she was keen enough to feel that something was wrong. As for that theory of Betty's insanity she scouted it with a harsh laugh whenever it was mentioned in her hearing. Betty—keen, sweet, trusting little Betty *insane*! Nonsense! It was unthinkable. If she was in a hospital anywhere she was there without warrant, and it behoved her faithful old nurse to find a way out for her. This she meant to do against all odds, for she was thoroughly aroused now.

She went to the window and looked down into the lighted street. Over there not four blocks away rose the steeple of the church where Betty had gone to be married! Around the corner was the great brick pile of the hospital where her stepmother said she had been taken from the church, and from which she was believed by the other servants to have escaped.

Standing thus looking out into the light-starred city, Candace began to form a plan, her plump tightly garmented chest rising and falling excitedly as she thought it all out. It was up to her to find out what had become of Betty. But how was she to get away without being suspected? Somehow she must do it. She knew perfectly the address that had been on that letter. She had written it down carefully from memory as soon as it had been taken away from her. She must go to Boston and find that man to whom it had been written, and discover whether he had ever received it. But she could not go until she found out certainly whether or not Betty had ever really escaped from the hospital. Who knew but that she was shut up there yet, and the madam telling this tale all about and advertising with a five-thousand-dollar reward! In the movies, too! Such a disgrace on the family! How the master would have writhed at the publicity of his beloved daughter—poor wee thing!

Candace turned from the window with her lips set, and tiptoeing to the door, listened. Yes, it was Aileen who was coming lightly up the stairs, singing in a low tone. It was Aileen's evening out. That menat that Marie would be more than usually active on the upper floor. She must manage it before Aileen left and Marie was called upstairs, or there would be no opportunity to get away without Marie seeing her.

Hastily she gathered her silk dress, her cloak, and her hat into a bundle with her purse and her gloves, and tied them into an old apron, with the strings hanging free. Then stealthily opening the window, she dropped them out into the kitchen area below, close to the region of the ash cans. It was a risk, of course, but one must take some chances, and the servants would all be in the kitchen just now, laughing and talking. They would scarcely have heard it fall.

She listened a tense instant, then closed the window, and possessing herself of few little things, gathered hastily about the room, which she could stuff in her pockets, she opened her door softly, closed it behind her, and trotted off down the stairs just as if she were going about her ordinary duty. Listening a minute outside the kitchen door she slipped stealthily down the cellar stairs, and tiptoed over to the area door where the ashman took out the ashes. Softly slipping the bolt she opened the door and drew in her bundle. Then standing within, she quickly slipped the black silk over her housemaid's gown, donned her coat and hat and gloves, and sallied forth. A moment more and she was in the next street with the consciousness that she might have done the like anytime sooner, if she'd wanted, in spite of that little spy-cat Marie.

"If I want to go back I'll just say I went after my insurance book," she chuckled to herself as she sped down the street in the direction of the hospital.

Arrived at the big building she asked to see the list of patients taken in on the day of Betty's wedding, and succeeded in getting a pretty accurate description of each one, sufficient at least to satisfy her that Betty was not among them. Then she asked a few more bold questions, and came away fully convinced that Betty had never been in that hospital.

By this time it was nine o'clock, and she meant to take the evening train for Boston, which left, she was sure, somewhere near midnight. She took a trolley to her old lodgings where she had been since Mrs. Stanhope had sent her away the first time, and hastily packed a small handbag with a few necessities, made a few changes in her garments, then went to see a fellow lodger whom she knew well, and where she felt sure she could easily get a check cashed, for she had a tidy little bank account of her own, and was well known to be reliable.

Having procured the necessary funds, she made her way to the station and found that she still had an hour to spare before the Boston train left.

Settled down at last in the back seat of a common car, she made herself as comfortable as her surroundings would allow, and gave herself up to planning the campaign that was before her.

Canny Candace did not go at once to the office of the brothers, James and George McIntyre, though she looked them up in the telephone book the very first thing when the train arrived in Boston even before she had had a bite to eat, and her cup of tea which meant more to her than the bite. She reasoned that they would be busy in the early hours and not be able to give her their undivided attention. She had not lived out all her life for nothing. She knew the ways of the world, and she had very strict ideas about the best ways of doing everything. So it happened that when she was at last shown into the office of the McIntyres, Warren Reyburn who had traveled to Boston on the sleeper of the same train that she had taken the night before, was just arising from an earnest conference with the two men. With her first glance, as the three emerged from the inner office, Candace saw that the two elder gentlemen were much disturbed and it flitted through her mind that she had come at an inopportune moment. Then her quick eye took in the younger man and her little alert head cocked to one side with a questioning attitude. Where had she seen him before? Candace had the kind of mind that kept people and events card-indexed even to the minutest detail, and it didn't take many seconds for her to place Warren Reyburn back in the church at the wedding, standing against the wall with his arms folded. She had noticed him particularly be-

cause he was so courteous to a little old lady who came in
too late to get a seat. She had studied him as he stood there,
waiting for the wedding march, and she had thought how
handsome he looked and how fine it would have been if her
wee Betty had been getting a man like that in place of the
weak-faced Bessemer Hutton. She had watched to see who
he was with, and felt deep satisfaction when she noticed
him lean over and speak to Mrs. Bryce Cochrane as if he
belonged to her. He wasn't her husband, because she knew
Mr. Cochrane, who had been a favorite with Mr. Stanhope
and much at the house. This man might be Mrs. Cochrane's
brother or the likes, and she had pleased herself watching
him till Betty arrived and took all her thoughts. So now she
stood with her little round head in its hectic hat tilted inter-
estedly to one side, watching, ears on the keen to catch any
word, for all the world like a bit brown sparrow saucily
perched on another man's window, where it really had no
right to be.

At last one of the McIntyre's shook hands gravely with the
younger man, and the other one attended him to the door,
talking in low tones. The McIntyre thus set at liberty,
turned questioningly toward the stranger, who was not slow
in getting to her feet and coming forward.

"You will maybe be Mr. James McIntyre?" she asked, lifting her sea-blue eyes set in her apple-red face, and fixing
her firm little lips in dignity. Candace was a servant and
knew her place, but she felt the importance of her mission,
and meant to have no disrespect done to it.

"I am Mr. George McIntyre," the gentleman replied,
and, indicating the man at the door, "Mr. James McIntyre
will be at liberty in a moment, but perhaps I will do as
well?"

Candace cocked a glance toward the elderly back at the
door; and then returned her look to Mr. George:

"You'll maybe be knowing Mr. Charles Stanhope?" she
propounded, as if she were giving him a riddle, and her
blue eyes looked him through and through:

"Oh, surely, surely! He was a very close friend! You—
knew him?"

"I was Miss Betty's nurse who cooked the griddle cakes for you the morning after the funeral——" she said, and waited with breathless dignity to see how he would take it.

"Oh! Is that so!" He beamed on her kindly. "Yes, yes, I remember those cakes. They were delicious! And what can I do for you? Just sit down. Why, bless me, I don't know but that your coming may be very opportune! Can you tell me anything of Miss Betty?"

Candace pressed her lips together with a knowing smile as much as to say she might tell volumes if it were wise, and she cast a glance at the other brother who was shaking hands now with his visitor and promising to meet him a little later:

"Yon man'll be knowing a bit, too, I'll be thinking," she hazarded nodding toward Reyburn as he left. "He was at the wedding, I'm most sure——!"

The elder McIntyre gave her a quick glance and signaled to his brother to come near:

"This is Miss Stanhope's nurse, the one who cooked breakfast for us at the time of the funeral," he said, and to Candace, "This is Mr. James McIntyre."

Candace fixed him with another of her inquisitive little glances:

"I've some bit papers put by that I thought ye might like to see," she said with a cautious air. "I've kept them fer long because I thought they might be wanted sometime, yet I've never dared bring them to your notice before lest I would be considered meddlin', and indeed I wasn't sure but you had them already. Will you please to look over them papers and see if you've ever seen them before?" She drew forth an envelope from her bag and handed it to them. "It's a bit letter that Mr. Stanhope wrote the day he was dyin' an' then copied and give to me to mail, and his lady took it away, sayin' she would attend to it. What I want to know is, did ye ever get the letter? If ye did it's all right and none of my business further, an' I'll go on my way back home again and think no more about it; but if ye didn't then there it is, an' you ought to see it, that's sure!"

The two men drew eagerly together and studied the trembling lines:

"It's his writing all right," murmured one, under his breath, and the brother nodded gravely:

"You say that this was the original of a letter that was given to you to mail to us?"

Candace nodded.

"It's what he wrote first, and got ink on it, an' then wrote it over. I can't say what changes he made, as I didn't read it, but this he gave to me to burn, and before I gets it burned my lady comes in and takes the letter from me while he was sleepin'; and so I hid the bit papers, thinkin' they might be a help to wee Betty sometime. And oh, can ye tell me anything of my little Lady Betty? Is she safe? Did she come to you for refuge? You needn't be afraid to tell me. I'll never breathe a word——!"

The two brothers exchanged quick glances of warning and the elder man spoke:

"My good woman, we appreciate your coming, and these papers may prove very useful to us. We hope to be able to clear up this matter of Miss Stanhope's disappearance very soon. She did not come to us, however, and she is not here. But if you will step into the room just beyond and wait for a little while we may be able to talk this matter over with you."

Very courteously he ushered the plump, apprehensive little woman into the next room and established her in an easy leather chair with a quantity of magazines and newspapers about her, but she kept her little head cocked anxiously on one side, and watched the door like a dog whose master has gone in and shut the way behind him; and she never sat back in her chair nor relaxed one iota during the whole of the two hours that she had to wait before she was called at last to the inner office where she found the handsome young man whom she remembered seeing at the wedding.

She presently found that Reyburn was as keen as he was handsome, but if she hadn't remembered him at the wedding as a friend of that nice Mrs. Cochrane, she never would have made it as easy as she did for him to find out things from her, for she could be canny herself on occasion if she tried, and she did not trust everybody.

Chapter 16

The mysterious disappearance of Candace from the Stanhope house caused nothing short of a panic. Herbert and his mother held hourly wrangles, and frantically tried one thing and then another. Day after day the responses came in from the advertisements they had caused to be put forth. Everyone was hotfoot for the reward, but so far little of encouragement had been brought out. More and more the young man was fixing his mind on the idea that Candace had something to do with Betty's disappearance, so he was leaving no stone unturned to find the nurse as well as the girl. To this end he insisted on seeing personally and cross-examining every person who came claiming to have a clue to the lost girl.

That morning, at about the same hour when Candace walked into the office of the McIntyre brothers in Boston, James, the butler, much against his dignity, was ushering a curious person into the presence of the son of the house. James showed by every line of his noble figure that he considered this duty beneath his dignity, and that it was only because the occasion was unusual that he tolerated it for a moment, but the man who ambled observantly behind him, stretching his neck to see everything that was to be seen in this part of the great house, that he might tell about it at the firehouse, failed to get the effect. He was wondering why in thunder such rich people as these seemed to be, couldn't afford carpets big enough to cover their whole floors, instead of just having skimpy little bits of pieces dropped around here and there, that made you liable to skid all over the place if you stepped on one of them biasly.

Herbert Hutton lifted his head and watched Abijah Gage slouch into the room. He measured him keenly and remained silent while Abijah opened up. There had been many other applicants for that reward that day, with stories cunningly woven, and facts, substantiated by witnesses, in one case a whole family brought along to swear to the fabrication; but as yet Herbert had not found a promising clue to his missing bride, and the time was going by. In a few days it would be too late, and his undisciplined spirit raged within him. It was not only his bride he wanted, it was her fortune, which was worth any trouble he might take; and every day, every hour, every minute now, it was slipping, slipping, slipping from his eager grasp.

Abijah was a little overawed in the presence of this insolent man of the world, but he felt he had, for almost the first time in his life, truth on his side, and he was strong in the power of it. With a cunning equal to the one that matched him he dealt out his information bit by bit, giving only enough at a time to make his victim sure it was the real thing this time; and then he halted stubbornly and would say no more until that five thousand dollars was signed and sealed over to him. They had a long argument, but in the end Bi won, and was given certain documents which he was satisfied would stand in court. A little later the telephone in Reyburn's office rang sharply, and when Jimmie Ryan responded a voice that he had never heard before asked for Mr. Warren Reyburn.

"He's out of town," Jimmy replied.

"How soon will he be back?" The voice was like a snarl.

"I'm not quite sure. He's called to Boston on business," swelled Jimmie loyally.

An oath ripped over the wire, and Jimmie raged within, and quailed. Was his idol then losing a great case?

"He might be back in a few hours," insinuated Jimmie. "Who shall I say called up if he should have me over long distance?"

"You needn't say anybody! I'll call up again," growled the voice, and the man hung up.

Jimmie sat for a long time in blissful reverie. "He's getting there!" he whispered to himself. "He'll get the big cases yet, and I can keep my first place. I must see Jane tonight and tell her."

Meanwhile, back at Tinsdale improvements had been going on at the Carsons. Bob, always handy with tools, had been putting in a tank over the bathtub. They had one at the house on the hill, only it was run by a windmill. Bob had a friend who was a plumber's son, and from him had obtained some lengths of secondhand water pipe and an old faucet. He had conceived the idea of a tank on the roof, and his first plan had been only a rainwater tank, but gradually as his vision widened he included a force pump in the outfit of desires. He hung around the plumbers until they unearthed an old force pump somewhat out of repair, and for a few days' assisting the plumber Bob acquired it, together with after-hour help to put it into operation. The next object was a tank, which seemed at first to represent the impossible; but the grocer at last offered a suggestion in the shape of several large empty hogsheads which he readily accepted at the price of four Saturday's work in the store.

All Bob's extra time was put into these improvements, and he was as excited every night when it grew dark and he was forced to come to supper because he couldn't see any longer to work, as if he had been building an airship.

The day the hogsheads were marshaled and connected and the force pump sent its first stream into them was a great occasion. The family assembled in the yard, with Elise Hathaway, who had been allowed to come over for a few minutes with Betty. Bob and his plumber friend pumped, and Emily climbed to the attic window, which overlooked the row of hogsheads, ranged so that the water would flow from one to the other, and acted as pilot to the new enterprise. As the first stream from the force pump, which Bob had lavishly painted red, crept its way up the pipes and began to wet the bottom of the first and highest hogshead Emily gave a little squeal of delight and shouted "It's come!

It's come! The water's come!" and the family below fairly held their breath with the wonder of it. Not that such a thing could be, but that their own freckled, grinning Bob should have been able to achieve it.

There was an elaborate system of tin conductors which conveyed the waste water from the bathtub out through a hole in the wall of the little laundry bathroom, and distributed it along the garden beds wherever its controller desired to irrigate. Thus the system became practical as well as a luxury. There was also an arrangement of gutter pipes for carrying off any surplus water from the hogsheads, so saving the Carson house from possible inundation at any time of heavy storms.

After the plumbing was finished Bob painted the laundry neatly inside with beautiful white paint and robin's-egg blue for the ceiling, and Betty told him it almost made one think of going swimming in the ocean. Next he began to talk about a shower bath. Betty told him what one was like and he began to spend more days down at the plumber's asking questions and picking up odd bits of pipe, making measurements, and doing queer things to an old colander for experiment's sake. The day that Warren Reyburn came for the first time Bob had the shower partly finished and ready to erect, and the next day saw it complete with a rod for the rubber curtain that Betty had promised to make for him. He and she were planning how they would make further improvements on the house before Jane and Nellie should come home for their summer vacation week. Betty had thoroughly entered into the life of the little household now, and was a part of it. She saved her own small wages, and grudged all she had to spend for necessary clothes, that she might contribute further to the comfort and beauty of the general home.

After Warren Reyburn's visit the last barrier between Betty and Ma seemed to be broken down. As soon as she had closed the door she flew into the other room and flung her arms around Ma's neck, bursting into soft weeping on her mothery shoulder. Ma had done a rapid turning act when she heard her coming, for in truth she had been peeping behind the green window shade to watch the handsome stranger go down the street, but she would have dropped the iron on her foot and pretended to be picking it up rather than let Betty suspect her interest in the visitor.

"Oh, Mother," she murmured in Mrs. Carson's willing ear, "I have been so frightened———"

"I know, dearie!" soothed the mother, quite as if she had been her own. "I know!"

"But he was very kind," she said lifting her head with an April effect of tears. "He's going to try to fix things for me so that I don't need ever to be afraid of anyone making trouble for me anymore. You see, I sort of ran away. There was somebody I was afraid of who troubled me a great deal."

"Yes, dearie, I thought as much," said Ma. "Jane kind of gave me to understand there was something like that. I'm real glad there's somebody goin' to look into your affairs an' fix things right for you. I knew you was restless an' worried. Now it'll get all straightened out. He's got a nice face. I trusted him first off. He's a church member, an' that's somethin'. They ain't all spiritual, but they're mostly clean an' just an' kindly, when they're anythin' at all but just plain hypocrites, which, thank the Lord, there ain't so many as some would have us believe. Now wash your face, dearie, an' run back to your place so you can come home early, for we're goin' to have the old hen with dumplin's for supper to celebrate."

That was one charming thing about that household: They celebrated every blessed little trifle that came into their lives, so that living with them was like a procession of beautiful thanksgivings.

It was while Betty was eating the gala "hen," delicious in its festive gravy and dumplings, that she looked off across the little dining room to the dark window with its twinkling village lights in the distance and thought of the stranger. A dark fear flashed across her sweet face and sparkled in the depths of her eyes for just an instant. Was it perhaps the distant bay of the hounds on her trail, coming nearer every moment? Then she remembered the heavenly Father and her newfound faith, and turned back to the cheery little room and the children's pleasant clatter, resolved to forget the fear and to trust all to Him who cared for her. Perhaps He had sent the pleasant stranger, and the thought brought a quiet little smile to settle about her lips. She laughed with Bob and Emily at how they had got wet with a sudden unexpected shower from the new bath while they were arranging the curtain on the rod, and Emily had turned the faucet on without knowing it. The patient-eyed mother watched them all and was satisfied.

How good it is that we cannot hear all the noises of the earth at the same time, nor know of every danger that lurks near as we are passing by! We grumble a great deal that God does not send us as much as we think He might, but we give scarce a thought to our escape from the many perils, lying close as our very breath, of which we never even dream.

At that moment, as they sat quietly eating their happy meal, a deadly particular peril was headed straight for Tinsdale.

Abijah Gage and Herbert Hutton boarded the evening train for Tinsdale together and entered the sleeper. Abijah shuffled behind, carrying the bags, a most extraordinary and humiliating position for him. He had never been known to carry anything, not even himself if he could help it, since the day his mother died and ceased to force him to carry in wood and water for her at the end of a hickory switch. He glanced uneasily round with a slight cackle of dismay as he arrived in the unaccustomed plush surroundings and tried to find some place to dump his load. But the well-groomed Herbert strode down the long aisle unnoticing and took possession of the section he had secured as if he owned the road.

"You can sit there!" he ordered Bi with a condescending motion, dropping into his own seat and opening a newspaper.

Bi sat down on the edge of the seat, and held on to the arm in a gingerly way as if he were afraid to trust himself to anything so different. He looked furtively up and down the car, eyed the porter, who ignored him contemptuously and finally came back and demanded his sleeper ticket with a lordliness that Bi did not feel he could take. But somehow the ticket got tangled in his pocket, and Bi had a hard time finding it, which deepened his indignation at the porter.

"I ain't takin' no sass from no one. My seat's paid fer all right," he said distinctly for the enlightenment of the other passengers, and Herbert Hutton reached out a discreet arm and dropped something in the porter's hand which sent him on his way and left Bi snorting audibly after him.

"You'd better shut up!" growled the dictator to Bi. "We don't want to be conspicuous, you know. If you can't hold your tongue and act as if you had ever traveled before, I'll get off this train at the next station and you can whistle for your reward. Do you understand?"

Bi dropped his toothless lower jaw a trifle and his little eyes grew narrow. This was no way to manage affable Bi. He loved a good visit, and he had counted on one all the way to Tinsdale. He had no idea of sitting silent.

"I understand," he drawled, "an' I'll be gormed ef I'll agree. I ain't told you yet where we get off, an' I don't have to ef I don't wantta. Ef you can't treat me like a gen'l'man you know where you can get off, an' I ain't havin' to state it."

Herbert Hutton drew his arrogant brows in a frown of annoyance, and whirled around to placate his guide:

"Now see here, you old popinjay, what's got into you?"

"No, sir, I ain't nobody's papa," babbled Bi, seeing he had scored a point. "I have enough to do to support myself without any family."

"That's all right, have it your own way, only shut up or we'll have somebody listening. Have a cigar. Take two. But you can't smoke 'em in here, you'll have to go to the smoking room. Wait! I'll see if we can get the drawing room."

The porter appeared and the change was effected, to the great disappointment of Bi, who kept continually poking his head out to get a glimpse of the fine ladies. He would much have preferred staying out in the main car and getting acquainted with people. His cunning had departed with the need. He had put things in the hands of this surly companion, and now he meant to have a good time and something to tell the gang about when he got home.

About midnight the train drew into a station and Herbert Hutton roused himself and looked out of the window. Bi, whose cunning had returned, followed his example. Suddenly he leaned forward excitedly and tapped the glass with a long finger:

"That's him! That's the guy," he whispered excitedly as another train drew in and passengers began to hurry down the platform and across to the waiting sleeper.

"Are you sure?"

"Sartin!"

"You mean the one with the coat over his arm, and the two men behind?" He stopped short with an exclamation.

Bi looked up cunningly. Now what was up? He saw a thundercloud on the face of his companion.

With embellishments Herbert Hutton asked if Bi had ever seen the two tall gray-haired men who were walking with their prey.

Bi narrowed his eyes and denied any knowledge, but perceived there were more sides than two to the enigma. Now, what could he figure out of those two guys? Were there more rewards to be offered? If so, he was a candidate. He wondered what chance there was of getting away from H.H. and sauntering through the train. He found, however, a sudden willingness on the part of his companion to vanish and let him do the scout work for the rest of the night.

With a sense of being on a vacation and a chance at catching big fish Bi swung out through the train. Bumping down among the now-curtained berths, adjusting his long form to the motion of the express, lurching to right and to left as they went round a curve, falling over an occasional pair of shoes and bringing down lofty reproaches from the sleepy porter, he penetrated to the day coaches and at last located his quarry.

They were sitting in a double seat, the younger man facing the two older ones, and had evidently been unable to get sleepers. Bi hung around the water cooler at the far end of the car until he had laid out his plans; then he sauntered up to the vacant seat behind the three men and dropped noiselessly into its depths, drawing his hat down well over his face, and apparently falling into instant slumber, with a fair sample of Tinsdale snoring brought in at moderate distances.

The conversation was earnest, in well-modulated voices, and hard to follow connectedly, for the men knew how to talk without seeming to the outside world to be saying anything intelligible. Occasionally a sentence would come out clear-cut in an interval of the rhythm of the train, but for the most part Bi could make little or nothing of it.

"In all the years we've been trustees of that estate we haven't seen her but twice," said one of the older men; "once at her father's second marriage, and again at his funeral. Then we only saw her at a distance. Her stepmother said she was too grief-stricken to speak with anyone, and it was by the utmost effort she could be present at the service."

"She looked very frail and young," said the other old man; "and her hair—I remember her hair!"

Bi changed his position cautiously and tried to peer over the back seat, but the voices were crowded together now, and the younger man was talking earnestly. He could not catch a syllable. "Trustees!" That word stayed with him. "Estate" was another promising one, and the fact that her hair had been remembered. He nodded his old head sagaciously, and later when the three men settled back in their seats more comfortably with their eyes closed he slid back to the water cooler and so on through the sleeper to the drawing room.

Hutton was sleeping the sleep of the unjust, which meant that he woke at the slightest breath, and Bi's breath was something to wake a heavier sleeper. So they sat and planned as the train rushed on through the night. Now and again Bi took a pilgrimage up to the day coach and back to report the three travelers still asleep.

About six o'clock in the morning the train slowed down, and finally came to a thrashing halt, waking the sleepers uncomfortably and making them conscious of crunching feet in the cinders outside, and consulting voices of trainmen busy with a hammer underneath the car somewhere.

Then they drowsed off to sleep again and the voices and hammering blended comfortably into their dreams.

The passengers in the day coach roused, looked at their watches, stretched their cramped limbs, squinted out to see if anything serious was the matter, and settled into a new position to sleep once more.

Bi, stretched for the nonce upon the long couch of the drawing room while his superior occupied the more comfortable berth, roused to instant action, slipped out to the platform and took his bearings. He had lived in that part of the country all his life and he knew where they ought to be by that time. Yes, there was the old sawmill down by Hague's Crossing, and the steeple over by the soft maple grove just beyond Fox Glove. It would not be a long walk, and they had a garage at Fox Glove!

He sauntered along the cinder path; discovered that the trouble with the engine was somewhat serious, requiring to wait for help, took a glimpse into the day coach ahead to assure himself that the three men were still asleep, and sauntered back to the drawing room.

His entrance roused the sleeper, who was on the alert instantly.

"Say, we got a hot box an' a broken engyne!" Bi announced. "It'll take us some time. We ain't far from Fox Glove. We could santer over an' git a car an' beat 'em to it!"

"We could?" said Hutton. "You sure? No chances, mind you!"

"Do it easy. Those guys are asleep. They won't get to the junction 'fore ten o'clock, mebbe later, an' they can't possibly get to our place 'fore 'leven."

"Lead the way!" ordered Hutton, cramming himself into his coat and hat.

"Better slide down on the other side," whispered Bi as they reached the platform. "We kin go back round the train an' nobody'll notice."

As if they had only come out to see what was the matter they idled along the length of the train around out of sight, slid down the bank, took a short cut across a meadow to a road, and were soon well on their way to Fox Glove in the early cool of the spring morning, a strangely mated couple bent on mischief.

Back on the cinder track the express waited, dreamily indifferent, with a flagman ahead and behind to guard its safety, and while men slept the enemy took wings and flew down the white morning road to Tinsdale, but no one ran ahead with a little red flag to the gray cottage where slept Betty, to warn her, though perchance an angel with a flaming sword stood invisibly to guard the way.

Chapter 17

Bob had just finished feeding the chickens when the automobile drew up at the door, and he hurried around the house to see who it might be. He was rather looking for the return of that nice lawyer again. He felt the family expected him sometime soon. Perhaps he would be to breakfast and Mother would want some fresh eggs.

They had dropped Bi at the edge of the village and there were only Hutton and the driver who had brought them. Bi had no mind to get mixed up in this affair too openly. He valued his standing in his hometown, and did not wish to lose it. He had an instinct that what he was doing might make him unpopular if it became known. Besides, he had another ax to grind.

Bob did not like the looks of the strange dark man who got out of the car and came into the yard with the air of a thrashing machine bolting into whatever came in his way. He stood sturdily and waited until he was asked who lived there, and admitted with a stingy "yes" that it was Mrs. Carson's house. A thundering knock on the front door followed, and the other man in the car got out and came into the yard behind the first.

"Well, you needn't take the door down," snapped Bob, and scuttled around the house to warn his mother, aware that he had been rude, and glad of it.

It was Betty who came to the door, for Ma was frying bacon and eggs for breakfast, and Bob hadn't been quite

soon enough. She started back with a scream, and eluding
the hand that reached for her arm, fairly flew back to the
kitchen, taking refuge behind Mrs. Carson, with her eyes
wild with fear and her hand on her heart, while Hutton
strode after her.

Mrs. Carson wheeled around with her knife in her hand
and faced him:

"What do you mean by coming into my house this way,
I'd like to know?" she demanded angrily, putting her arm
around Betty.

"I beg your pardon," said Hutton, a poor apology for cour-
tesy slipping into his manner. "I don't suppose you know it,
but that is my wife you are harboring there, and she ran
away from home several months ago! I have just discovered
her whereabouts and have come to take her away!"

Ma straightened up with the air of a queen and a judge,
while Betty stifled a scream and in a small voice full of terror cried: "It isn't true, Mrs. Carson, it isn't true! Oh,
Mother, don't let him take me!"

Mrs. Carson pushed Betty behind her, the knife still in
her other hand, and answered with dignity:

"You've made a big mistake, Mr. Herbert Hutton; this
isn't your wife at all. I know all about you."

Hutton put on a look of instant suavity.

"Oh, of course, madam, she has told you that, but I'm
sorry to have to tell you that she is not in her right mind.
She made her escape from the mental hospital."

"Oh, rats!" shouted Bob, and vanished out the kitchen
door, slamming it behind him.

Emily, frightened and white, stood just outside, and he
nearly knocked her over in his flight. He pulled her along
with him, whispering in her ear excitedly:

"You beat it down to the fire gong and hit it for all you're
worth! Quick!"

Emily gave him one frightened look and sprang to action.
Her little feet sped down the path to the lot where hung the
big fire gong, like two wild rabbits running for their lives,
and in a moment more the loud whang of alarm rang
through the little town, arousing the "gang" and greatly dis-

concerting Bi, who was craning his neck at the station and watching the fast-growing speck down the railroad track. That sure was the train coming already. How had they made it so soon?

But Bob was on his stomach in the road scuttling the ship that was to have carried away the princess. The chauffeur was fully occupied in the house, for he had been ordered to follow and be ready to assist in carrying away an insane person, and he had no thought for his car at present. It was an ugly job, and one that he didn't like, but he was getting big pay, and such things had to be done.

Bob's knife was sharp. He always kept it in good condition. It did many of the chores about the house, and was cunning in its skill. It cut beautiful long punctures in the four tires, until there was no chance at all of the car's going on its way for some time to come. Then he squirmed his way out on the opposite side from the house, slid along by the fence to the side door, around to the back like a flash and without an instant's hesitation hauled up his elaborate system of drainage. He stuck the longest conductor pipe through the open window of the old laundry, clutched at the sill and swung inside, drawing the pipe in after him.

The altercation in the kitchen had reached white heat. Hutton's suavity was fast disappearing behind a loud angry tone. He had about sized up Ma and decided to use force.

It was a tense moment when Bob, his hasty arrangements made, silently swung open the laundry door in full range of the uninvited guests and waited for the psychological moment. Mrs. Carson had dropped her knife and seized the smoking hot frying pan of bacon as a weapon. She was cool and collected, but one could see in her eyes the little devil of battle that sometimes sat in Bob's eyes as she swung the frying pan back for a blow. Suddenly out flashed a cold steel eye, menacing, unanswerable, looking straight into her own.

At that instant, unannounced and unobserved, through the laundry door lumbered a long ugly tin conductor pipe, and the deluge began. Straight into the eyes of the would-be husband it gushed, battering swashingly down on the cocked revolver, sending it harmlessly to the floor, where it added to the confusion by going off with a loud report, and sending the chauffeur to the shelter of the parlor. Bob never knew how near he came to killing someone by his nasty service, and Ma never had the heart to suggest it. Instead she acted promptly and secured the weapon before the enemy had time to recover from the shock.

Bob, in the laundry, standing on a chair mounted on a board across the bathtub, sturdily held his wobbling conductor pipe and aimed it straight to the mark. Of course he knew that even a well-filled phalanx of hogsheads could not hold the enemy forever, but he was counting on the fire company to arrive in time to save the day.

Gasping, clawing the air, ducking, diving here and there to escape the stream, Herbert Hutton presented a spectacle most amusing and satisfying to Bob's boy mind.

"Beat it, Lizzie, beat it! Beat it!" he shouted above the noise of the pouring waters. But Betty, white with horror, seemed to have frozen to the spot. She could not have moved if she had tried, and her brain refused to order her to try. She felt as if the end of everything had come and she were paralyzed.

Down the street with dash and flourish, licking up excitement like a good meal, dashed the gang, the fire chief ostentatiously arraying himself in rubber coat and helmet as he stood on the side of the engine, while the hysterical little engine bell banged away, blending with the sound of the bell of the incoming train at the station. Bi, with his mouth stretched wide, and one foot holding him for the train while the other urged toward the fire and excitement, vibrated on the platform, a wild figure of uncertainty. Where duty and inclination both called, cupidity still had the upper hand.

For once Bi did not have to act a part as he stood watching the three travelers descend from the train. The excitement in his face was real and his gestures were quite natural, even the ones made by his one and only long waving toplock of gray hair that escaped all bounds as his hat blew off with the suction of the train. Bi rushed up to the three men wildly:

"Say, was you goin' down to Carson's house after that Hope girl?" he demanded loudly.

The three men surveyed him coldly, and the young one gave him a decided shove:

"That will do, my friend," he said firmly. "We don't need any of your assistance."

"But I got a line on this thing you'll want to know," he insisted, hurrying alongside. "There's a guy down there in a car goin' to take her away. He ain't been gone long, but you won't find her 'thout my help. He's goin' to take her to a insane institution. I let on I was helpin' him an' I found out all about it."

"What's all this?" said Reyburn, wheeling about and fixing the old fellow with a muscular young shake that made his toothless jaws chatter. "How long ago did he go? What kind of a looking man was he?"

"Lemme go!" whined Bi, playing to make time, one cunning eye down the road. "I ain't as young as I used to be, an' I can't stand gettin' excited. I got a rig here a purpose, an' I'll take you all right down, an' then ef he's gone, an' I s'pose he must be, 'cause your train was late, why, we'll foller."

"Well, quick, then!" said Reyburn, climbing into the shackley spring wagon that Bi indicated, the only vehicle in view. The two trustees climbed stiffly and uncertainly into the backseat as if they felt they were risking their lives, and Bi lumbered rheumatically into the driver's place and took up the lines. It appeared that the only living thing in Tinsdale that wasn't awake and keen to go to the fire was that horse, and Bi had to do quite a little urging with the stump of an old whip. So, reluctantly, they joined the procession toward the Carson house.

As the stream from the hogshead gurgled smaller, and the victim writhed out of its reach and began to get his bearings, suddenly the outside kitchen door burst open and a crew of rubber-coated citizens sprang in, preceded by a generous stream of chemicals which an ardent young member of the company set free indiscriminately in his excitement. It struck the right man squarely in the middle and sent him sprawling on the floor.

Bob dropped the conductor pipe in exhausted relief and flew to the scene of action. It had been fearful to be held from more active service so long. Emily, outside, could be seen dancing up and down excitedly and directing the procession, with frightened shouts, "In there! In the kitchen! Quick!" as the neighbors and townsmen crowded in and filled the little kitchen demanding to know where the fire was.

Mrs. Carson with dignity stepped forward to explain:

"There ain't any fire, friends, an' I don't know how you all come to get here, but I reckon the Lord sent you. You couldn't a-come at a better moment. We certainly was in some trouble, an' I'll be obliged to you all if you'll just fasten that man up so't he can't do any more harm. He came walkin' in here tryin' to take away a member of my family by force, an' he pointed this at me!"

She lifted the incriminating weapon high where they could all see.

Herbert Hutton, struggling to his feet in the crowd, began to understand that this was no place for him, and looked about for an exit, but none presented itself. The chauffeur had vanished and was trying to make out what had happened to his car.

Hutton, brought to bay, turned on the crowd like a snarling animal, although the effect was slightly spoiled by his drabbled appearance, and roared out insolently:

"The woman doesn't know what she's talking about, men; she's only frightened. I came here after my wife, and I intend to take her away with me! She escaped from a hospital some time ago, and we've been looking for her ever since. This woman is doing a very foolish and useless thing in resisting me, for the law can take hold of her, of course."

The crowd wavered and looked uncertainly at Mrs. Carson and at Betty cowering horrified behind her, and Hutton saw his advantage:

"Men," he went on, "there is one of your own townsmen who knows me and can vouch for me. A Mr. Gage. Abijah Gage. If you will just look him up—he was down at the station a few minutes ago. He knows that all I am saying is true!"

A low sound like a rumble went over the little audience and they seemed to bunch together and look at one another while some kind of an understanding traveled from eye to eye. An articulate syllable, "Bi!" breathed in astonishment, and then again "Bi!" in contempt. Public opinion, like a panther crouching, was forming itself ready to spring, when suddenly a new presence was felt in the room. Three strangers had appeared and somehow quietly gotten into the doorway. Behind them, stretching his neck and unable to be cautious any longer, appeared Bi's slouching form. Crouching public opinion caught sight of him and showed its teeth, but was diverted by the strangers.

Then suddenly, from the corner behind Ma, slipped Betty with outstretched hands, like a lost thing flying to its refuge, straight to the side of the handsome young stranger.

He put out his hands and drew her to his side with a protecting motion, and she whispered:

"Tell them, please; oh, make them understand."

Then Reyburn, with her hand still protectingly in his, spoke:

"What that man has just said is a lie!"

Hutton looked up, went deadly white and reeled as he saw the two elderly men.

The crowd drew a united breath and stood straighter, looking relieved. Bi blanched, but did not budge. Whatever happened he was in with both crowds. Reyburn continued:

"I carry papers in my pocket which give authority to arrest him. If the sheriff is present will he please take charge of him. His name is Herbert Hutton, and he is charged with trying to make this lady marry him under false pretenses in order to get control of her property. She is not his wife, for she escaped before the ceremony was performed. I know, for I was present. These two gentlemen with me are the trustees of her estate."

Estate!

The neighbors looked at Betty respectfully.

Bi dropped his jaw perceptibly and tried to figure out how that would affect him. The sheriff stepped forward to magnify his office, and the silence was impressive, almost reverent. In the midst of it broke Bob's practical suggestion:

"Shut him in the coal shed. It's got a padlock an' is good an' strong. He can't kick it down."

Then the law began to take its course, the fire gang stepped out, and Mrs. Carson set to work to clean up. In the midst of it all Reyburn looked down at Betty, and Betty looked up at Reyburn, and they discovered in some happy confusion that they still had hold of hands. They tried to cover their embarrassment by laughing, but something had been established between them that neither could forget.

Chapter 18

The days that followed were full of bliss and peace to Betty. With Hutton safely confined in the distant city, and a comfortable sum of her accumulated allowance in the Tinsdale bank, with a thorough understanding between herself and her trustees and the knowledge that her estate was large enough to do almost anything in reason that she wished to do with it, and would be hers in three weeks, life began to take on a different look to the poor storm-tossed child. The days in the Carson home were all Thanksgivings now, and every member of the family was as excited and happy as every other member. There were arguments long and earnest between Betty and her benefactor as to how much she might in reason be allowed to do for the family now that she had plenty of money, but in the end Betty won out, declaring that she had wished herself on this family in her distress, and they took her as a man does when he marries, for better for worse. Now that the worse had passed by she was theirs for the better, and she intended to exercise the privilege of a daughter of the house for the rest of her natural life.

Bi Gage was worried. He was still trying to get something out of the estate for his part in the exercises, and he vibrated between Tinsdale and Warren Reyburn's office working up his case. The five-thousand-dollar reward was as yet unpaid, and the papers he held didn't seem to impress the functionaries nearly so much as he had expected. It began to look as though Bi had missed his chances in life once more, and when he took his old seat in the firehouse and smoked, he said very little. Popular opinion was still crouching with her eye in his directon and it behooved him to walk cautiously and do nothing to offend. So while he smoked he cogitated in his cunning little brain, and hatched out a plan by which he might get in with the heiress later, perhaps, when things had quieted down a little and she had her money.

Betty received a pitiful letter from her stepmother, trying to explain away her part in the affair and professing to be so relieved at the news that Betty was still alive and well that she cared nothing about anything else, not even the fact that poor dear Herbert was landed in jail, or that the fortune which she had schemed so long to keep in her own power was wrested from her so ignominiously. She begged Betty to come back to their home and "be happy again together."

But Betty was so happy where she was that she could afford to be generous and try to forget her wrongs. She wrote a decent little note gently but firmly declining to come "home" ever again, making it quite plain that she was no longer deceived by honeyed phrases, and closing with a request that if in future in communication might be necessary it should be made through her lawyer, Mr. Warren Reyburn.

This same Warren Reyburn had returned to his city office in a very much exalted state of mind. He could not get away from that little hand of Betty's that had been laid so tremblingly and confidingly in his; and yet how could he, a poverty-stricken lawyer with absolutely no prospects at all, ever dare to think of her, a lady of vast estates. Still, there was some comfort in the fact that he had still some business to transact for her, and would have to return to Tinsdale again. He might at least see her once more. So he solaced himself on his return trip, feeling that he had done some good work, and that he would have a pleasant report to give to Jane Carson when he called upon her, as he meant to do the next day.

He arrived at home to find James Ryan in a great state of excitement. A pile of mail had arrived, and he had memorized the return addresses on the outside of all the envelopes. One was from a big corporation, and another bore a name widely spoken of in the circles of the world of finance, Jimmie in close council with Jane Carson, had decided that it must be from that person who called up twice on the phone and swore such terrible oaths when he found that Reyburn was away.

Jimmie hovered nervously about, putting things to rights, while Reyburn read his mail. He had come to the smallest envelope of all, a plain government envelope now, and nothing had developed. Jimmie saw his first place fast slipping away from him and his heart grew heavy with fear. Perhaps after all nothing good had turned up yet.

Suddenly Reyburn sprang up and came toward him with an open letter, holding out his hand in a joyous greeting:

"Read that, Ryan! We're made at last, and I shan't have to let you go after all!"

Ryan read, the letters dancing before his delighted eyes, every one wearing an orange blossom on its brow. It was from an old established and influential firm, asking Reyburn to take full charge of all their law business, and saying they had been referred to him by two old friends in Boston, who by the way were Betty's two trustees.

"Come on, Ryan, come out to lunch with me! We've got to celebrate," said Reyburn. "I have a hunch somehow that you have been the one that brought me this good luck. You and a Miss Jane Carson. You both share alike, I guess, but you were the first with your five-thousand-dollar reward story."

"Jane Carson!" said Jimmie mystified. "Why, *she's* my *girl*!"

"Your girl?" said Reyburn, a queer look coming in his eyes. "You don't say! Well, you're in some luck, boy, with a girl like that! And, by the way, next time you see her, ask her to show you her wedding dress!"

And not another word would Reyburn tell him, though he recurred frequently to the subject during the very excellent lunch which they had together in friendly companionship.

They spent the afternoon composing the brief and comprehensive letter in response to the momentous one of the morning, and in the evening together they sought out Jane Carson, Reyburn staying only long enough to outline the ending of the Elizabeth Stanhope story, while Jimmie remained to hear the beginning, and get a glimpse of the wedding gown, which Reyburn assured Jane he was sure she need never return. He said he thought if the owner of it was married ever in the future she would be likely to want a gown that had no unpleasant associations.

Great excitement prevailed in Tinsdale as the weeks went by. Betty had bought the lots either side of the Carson house, and wonderful improvements were in progress. A windmill was being erected and water pipes laid scientifically. Workmen arrived, some of them from the village, some from the city. Extensive excavations went on about the old house, and stone arrived. It began to be whispered about that "Miss Stanhope," as Betty was now called, was going to build the house all over and all of stone.

The work went forward rapidly as work can go when there is money enough behind it, and the family, living in the little old part of the house, and still using the faithful tin bathtub and shower of Bob's manufacture, now looked forward to real bathrooms on the bedroom floor, with tiled floors and porcelain fittings. Large windows cropped out on the new walls that were going up, a wide stone chimney and porches. A charming little stone affair in the back yard that went up so quietly it was hardly noticed until it was done suddenly became the home of a big gray car that arrived in town one morning. Betty gave up her position at the Hathaways' so that she could have more time to superintend the work and see that it was just as she wanted it, and she and Bob spent hours going over the plans together, he making many wise suggestions. Mrs. Hathaway called her "Miss Stanhope" with elaborate ceremony, and made Elise kiss her whenever she met her.

Betty went to a nearby town and bought some pretty clothes, and a lot of things for Ma and Emily and Bob. A beautiful new piano came by express and took the place of Mrs. Barlow's tinpanny one.

Then Betty went up to the city and bought more things, furniture and silver and curtains and rugs, and brought Jane back with her to take a rest and see the little old house once more before it became the big new house, and stay until she was ready to be married; for Betty was determined to have the house ready for Jane's wedding.

When all the new beautiful things began to arrive Betty told Ma that she had taken her in when she was poor and homeless and absolutely penniless, and now all these things were her reward, and Betty couldn't do enough ever to thank her for what she had done for her. They had offered a five-thousand-dollar reward for news of her, and Ma had done more than ten thousand and thousands of thousands of dollars' worth of holding back news about her, and she was never going to get done giving her her reward.

Of course Betty brought Nellie home, too, and established her in a lovely new room just fit for a young girl, and began to pet her and fix her up with pretty things as any loving sister might do if she had money of her own.

All this time Reyburn had much business to transact in Tinsdale, for Betty had asked him to look after all the little details about the building for her, and he had to come down every weekend and look things over to see that she was not being cheated. And once he brought Jimmie down with him for Ma to look over and approve and they had a wonderful time with the two best hens in the hencoop for dinner. Ryan incidentally gave his approval to Betty.

During these visits Reyburn was making great strides in the wisdom and the knowledge of the love of God. One could not be in that family over Sunday and not feel the atmosphere of a Christian home. Even Jimmie felt it and said he liked it; that he wanted his home to be that way when he had one. He went obediently to church with Jane, and marveled at the way social classes were getting all muddled up in his world.

The Christmas time was coming on when the house finally got itself completed and was ready for living, and with holly and mistletoe and laurel they made it gay for the wedding. Betty spent several days with Jane in New York picking out Jane's "trooso" things, and then a few more days doing some shopping of her own, and at last the wedding day arrived.

Nobody thought it queer, though Jimmie felt just the least bit shy when the two trustees of Betty's estate arrived the night before from Boston and incorporated themselves into the wedding party. Ma seemed to think it was all right, so nobody said anything about it.

But after the ceremony when Jane and Jimmie were happily married, Jane looking very young and pretty indeed in Betty's old wedding gown, veil and slippers and all, and standing under the holly bell in the laurel arch to be congratulated just as it had been arranged, there suddenly came a hush over everybody. Jane noticed for the first time that Betty was not anywhere in the room. Then everybody's eyes went to the wide staircase, and here came Betty trailing down the stairs on the arm of Reyburn, wearing still the little white organdie she had worn a few minutes before as a bridesmaid, only she had thrown aside the rose-colored sash and put over her brow a simple tulle veil, and her arms were full of little pink rosebuds and lilies of the valley.

Up they walked in front of the minister just where the others had stood, and were married with the same sweet simple service, and everybody was so surprised and delighted and excited and breathless that Bob simply couldn't stand it. He slipped into the little music room where the piano had been installed, turning a handspring on the floor, and then sat down and played chopsticks on the piano with all the pedals on, till Ma had to send Emily in to stop him.